STARSLAVE

On several settled worlds of the Earth Confederation, towns had been destroyed by attacking alien vessels. Captain Kurt Varl was the only man to have fought an alien ship and destroyed it — the only survivor from a crew of thirty. He must lead another ship and crew into battle, knowing that as well as the alien raiders, he faced the things that lurked in limbo, existing in four dimensions and capable of transforming humans into things of screaming horror . . .

E. C. TUBB

STARSLAVE

Complete and Unabridged

LINFORD
Leicester

First published in Great Britain

First Linford Edition
published 2010

Copyright © 2009 by E. C. Tubb

British Library CIP Data

Tubb, E. C.
    Starslave. - - (Linford mystery library)
    1. Space colonies- -Fiction. 2. Space warfare
    - -Fiction. 3. Science fiction.
    4. Large type books.
    I. Title II. Series
    823.9'14–dc22

    ISBN 978–1–44480–459–1

Published by
F. A. Thorpe (Publishing)
Anstey, Leicestershire

Set by Words & Graphics Ltd.
Anstey, Leicestershire
Printed and bound in Great Britain by
T. J. International Ltd., Padstow, Cornwall

This book is printed on acid-free paper

1

In the shadows the figure was tall, slender, touched with glitters, hung with the scent of expensive perfume. A harlot or a bored lady of quality seeking nocturnal pleasure — on Ceruti during carnival both were common. Her voice was a husky contralto.

'Varl? Captain Kurt Varl?'

He halted, narrowing his eyes, seeing no more than before. Standing against an elaborate filigree of coloured light she was little more than a silhouette; a shape embraced by the curved walls of the alcove holing the illuminated screen. Then, from a point high in the sky, chemical fire burst in a shower of scintillant rain that dispelled the night and banished the shadows. In its glow he saw an embroidered cloak, a headdress of metallic feathers framing the pale ovoid of a face. One slashed with the scarlet of a generous mouth, illuminated by silvered eyes.

'Please — you are Captain Varl?'

'And if I am?'

'Then you are fortunate. Come!' A hand lifted in an imperious gesture. The other, hidden within the cloak, moved a little as if changing its grasp on the fabric. 'Come closer, Kurt. Taste the sweet joy of Carnival. Tonight will be one you will never forget.'

A routine promise yet the voice held more than the ritual lure. Varl hesitated, looking to either side, scanning the straggle of pedestrians, the hovercar that had come to rest a few paces distant.

'You don't trust me?' She stepped from the alcove to stand before him. Her perfume caressed his nostrils and he saw his own image reflected from the silvered eyes scant inches below his own. Smiling she said, 'Would it make you feel more comfortable if I set a price?'

'For what?'

'Need I explain?' Her laughter matched the music of her voice. 'For food and wine and entertaining company. For surprise and excitement — and perhaps something more. Am I so ugly you must turn away?' She stepped even closer so that he could hear the rustle of the cloak over her body. Then, quickly, before he could speak or respond, she added, 'I need an escort. One to accompany me to a party. To protect me if I should need protection.'

'Against violence?'

'Against boredom. Come.' Her hand rested on his arm. 'Please, Captain, be generous. Accommodate me. Help me to win the prize.'

A game, he guessed, a treasure hunt of some kind in which each had to return with a selected companion; a mute, a trader, a spacer, a scavenger. She had drawn the need to find a rarer item — but how had she known his name?

'It was on the card,' she explained when he asked. 'That together with your description. The computer said you had recently arrived on Ceruti and where you were living. I simply chose to wait where I guessed you would venture.' Her hand closed on his in the gloom of the cab they had hired. The driver didn't turn as she pressed herself against her companion.

Beneath the cloak she was almost naked. 'Kurt! Kurt — kiss me!'

The car halted before he could oblige.

It had taken them to a building on the edge of town; a sombre place with shrouded windows and stairs that climbed to a solid door. It opened as they neared, light streaming to slash the night, music throbbing from somewhere within.

'Edallia!' The man within stepped forward, smiling, eyes moving from the woman to her companion. 'So you found him. Good!'

'Let us in, Paul.'

He stepped aside, still smiling, his eyes hungry as he stared at Varl. A man broad in his shoulders, thick in his arms, dressed in a barbaric costume of straps and gilded plates, a dagger hanging at his side. He slammed shut the door as Varl followed Edallia into the house and he heard the rasp of closing bolts. Then the music swelled louder to accompany a babble of greeting and a girl came towards him, smiling, wearing little but paint, a brimming goblet in her hands.

'To you, Edallia!' She drank. 'To us all!'

She drank again then, tensing, said, 'To you, Captain. This to — '

'No!' Edallia stepped before her, cloak swirling as she stripped it from her shoulders. 'Take this, Maya. Give me the goblet — here!' She turned towards Varl as the girl left with the cloak. Her costume was brief as he'd known; straps and plates to adorn her flesh. Gilded decoration for a body that was superb.

She smiled as he looked at her, lifting the goblet to stain her lips with its contents, a rich purple that gave the natural scarlet a deeper hue and tinged her teeth with the hint of blood.

'Here!' She handed him the goblet. 'The wine I promised you. The music you can hear. There is food for the taking and, as for the rest — ' Her inhalation lifted her breasts to thrust them hard against the metallic cups caressing their contours. 'To the victor the spoils, Kurt. Isn't that the way it goes?'

'What have I won?'

'As yet nothing. But the night is still young and much can happen. In the meantime look around, enjoy yourself.

Let them all see you. Touch you. Revel in your presence. Sabatova! Dance with me!'

She was gone, weaving in a complicated rhythm with an ebon giant adorned with red and yellow and dangling bones. A make-believe savage as she was a make-believe barbarian queen and yet there was nothing artificial in the way they moved each muscle responding to the pulse of the music, each movement the symbolic depiction of an age-old rite.

One which affected the others so that, within minutes, the room was full of weaving shapes, the air heavy with the meaty slap of naked feet on the boards, the beat of hands on thighs and hips and buttocks.

A demonstration of primitive abandon that Varl watched before moving around the chamber.

It was large, set, he guessed, in the rear of the house, the windows sealed with metal plates. A table flanked one side bearing a choice of foods and he selected a cake and ate it, taking a sip of wine before picking up a small pastry roll filled with a meaty, succulent paste. A second table held a variety of bottles. A third bore a host of crushed pods, which accounted for the scent of ka'sense hanging in the air. Other odours were not so familiar and he guessed at the presence of uninhibiting vapours and sensual stimulants. Common additions to any party especially a fancy-dress one and he felt out of place. Among the near-nudity of the dancers and their barbaric splendour his own, normal clothing made him as conspicuous as a raven among peacocks.

Too conspicuous — had Edallia told the truth there should have been others. Or had he been the sole target of the treasure hunt?

The dance was nearing a climax, the music deafening as it climbed to a crescendo of emotive sound. None noticed as he reached the door. The passage was apparently empty; an illusion broken as he neared the door.

'Going somewhere, Captain?' Paul smiled without humour as he lifted the gun in his hand. 'The party isn't over yet.'

'It is for me.'

'No.' Paul shook his head, the gun remaining steady. 'That's where you're wrong. You can't leave yet. You see, Captain — you are the party.' His tone hardened. 'Go back to the room now. Back, you bastard, before I burn a hole in your guts!'

The music died as Varl obeyed, the recorder switching to another rhythm, one softer, more subtle than the other. Faces stared at him as he stepped into the chamber, Paul following behind, the laser aimed at his back. A touch and it would vent a stream of searing energy that would cut and pierce like a burning sword.

As they entered he explained, 'He tried to get away.'

'And you stopped him, Paul. That was clever of you.' Edallia came forward, smiling, a hand outstretched. 'I'll handle this. Give me the gun.' Then, as he hesitated, she snapped, 'The gun, damn you!'

'I've a right — '

'We all have a right!' Sabatova, skin glistening with sweat, snarled his anger.

'Give her the gun.' Then, as he obeyed. 'Kill the music. Let's get on with doing what we gathered to do.'

'Kill him!' Screamed a woman. 'Kill — '

'Wait!' Sabatova lifted a hand for silence. Looking at Varl he said, 'You admit to being Captain Kurt Varl?'

'I don't deny it.'

'Of the *Odile*?'

'The *Odile* is dead.'

'And so is everyone who rode in her!' The shout was an accusing scream. 'Only you survived, you bastard! How does it feel to have killed so many?'

'Duty killed them.'

'You scum! You gave the orders!'

'I held the command,' admitted Varl. 'They died and now you want to kill me. For what reason? Revenge?' He stared at the faces ringing him, savage in their paint and adornment, but belonging to those who had been civilised too long. 'Is that what you want? Revenge?'

'You've been tried,' said a woman. 'Found guilty of having betrayed those who trusted you. A master should die with his men.'

9

'And women!' The voice was harsh, brittle. 'Don't forget the women!'

'Elsa Hoetmar,' said Sabatova. 'He was to have married her.' He pointed. 'That's Ellain Ovideo — remember him? She does. It isn't easy for forget a brother. And that's Ivan Yegorovich and he is Brian Cachou and she is the sister of Lucy Bland and — '

Varl said, harshly, 'The *Odile* carried a crew of thirty — are you going to name them all?'

'They're dead.'

'Did you expect them to live forever?'

'My God!' A woman thrust herself forward to stare at Varl. 'I've heard of people like you,' she said bitterly, 'but I never believed any really existed. You animal! You should be in a cage!'

She was dressed in paint and beads with decorated bands supporting sagging breasts and bulging hips. Her teeth, stained red and painted to simulate filed points, framed a blotched tongue. Her eyes held madness. Her breath stank of wine and drugs.

'An animal?' Varl met her eyes his own

10

betraying his contempt and anger. 'You call me that? You freakish bitch, look at yourself.'

'Bastard!'

She threw herself towards him, hands lifted, fingers curved into claws. Her nails were filed into points, long, threatening his eyes. They slashed down, missing as he moved backwards, then the meaty slap of his hand against her mouth cut short her frenzied shrieking.

'He hit me!' She looked at the blood dappling her torso, the hand she lifted to her split lips. 'He hit me!'

'Get him!' A man yelled from the back of the crowd. 'Tear him apart!'

'Wait!' The woman who had mentioned the trial lifted her arm. A gilded snake wreathed the flesh. 'We sat in judgment and a decision was made. We — '

'Kill!' yelled the man again. 'What are we waiting for? Kill the swine! Kill!'

Varl backed as the ring closed in. Hours earlier they had been peaceful citizens conditioned into a civilised mould. Hours later they would be the same but, now, they were acting the parts they had adopted. Barbarians lusting for blood — his.

He moved as Sabatova lunged forward to stand before him, legs braced, fist bunched and poised to strike. His voice was a bellow of triumph.

'I'll take him. To me the task of execution. In the name of Sam Mboto, you scum, die!'

He grunted as Varl lunged forward, ducking beneath the piston-blow of the fist to send his shoe rasping against a naked, glistening shin. A blow followed by the thrust of his left hand at the genitals and then, as Sabatova doubled, his right arm slammed upwards, the hand bent back at an angle from the wrist, the heel of his palm hitting the jaw with bone-breaking force.

Another followed the giant as he fell, gagging, one hand to his bruised larynx as he fought to breathe. A woman screamed as an elbow pulped her nose then Varl was at the table holding the bottles.

'The gun!' Paul yelled from where he stood at the rear of the crowd. 'Use the gun, Edallia! Burn him down!'

He snarled as she made no motion to obey, snatching the dagger from his belt and throwing it with a sweep of his arm. Varl saw the glitter, moved, felt the burn as the point ripped open his cheek and threw the bottle in his hand. A missile that struck Paul's temple and sent him down. Another followed to crash against the far wall and then it was too late to throw more, the crowd had pressed too close.

Animals baying for his life.

Varl turned to face them, closing his eyes as he smashed the bottles he held together, opening them as the shards fell to leave him with the necks in his hands, the crude hilts ringed with vicious points of broken glass.

'You'll get me,' he snarled. 'Try hard enough and you'll get me — but I'll cut the first few to come close. Who will it be?' He moved, swaying from side to side on balanced feet, the jagged weapons in his hand lifting to point, to slash, to threaten. 'Two at least,' he said. 'Maybe more — which of you will be first?'

He lunged without waiting for an

answer, sending a shard of glass to cut a furrow over a naked chest, following it with a jab which sent blood to bubble from the belly of another. A woman backed as the points stabbed at her eyes, a man spun to gain distance and, suddenly, Varl stood in a cleared space.

'That's better.' He moved forward, sidling around the chamber so as to protect his back. 'I'm leaving. Get away from that door. One of you open the outer portal.'

'I'll do it.' Edallia smiled as she made the promise. 'And I'll come with you. Hurry, darling.'

A woman with a gun, he hadn't forgotten, but she had had no attempt to use it and both hands were empty. Once the way was clear he would make sure it wouldn't be used.

He completed the journey to the door, passed through it, backed down the passage to where she was waiting. He heard the rasp of bolts and the creak of hinges. The touch of cool, night air dried the sweat on his neck. Turning he saw her near-naked beauty framed against the outer darkness.

'Darling!' Her hands lifted, empty, the rise of her arms emphasising the contours of her breasts. 'Darling you were magnificent! A true warrior. And, to the victor, the spoils. Remember?'

'Stand aside.'

'You won, darling. Don't you understand? You won and have a right to claim your prize.' She stepped closer towards him, a vision of loveliness, febrile with barbaric splendour. 'Hold me, Kurt. Take me.'

She halted an inch from the points aimed at her flesh, frowning, head lowered a little, the metallic feathers of her headdress a spined ridge beneath his eyes. Behind he sensed watching eyes. Beyond her lay the safety of the night.

'Move,' he said. 'Damn you — move!'

She obeyed, stepping backwards, head lifting, then he heard the thin, spiteful buzz, felt the prick of the dart which had spurted from her headdress to bury itself in his throat. A moment in which he tried to lift the bottles and ruin the perfection of her breasts and face and belly, then he was down, paralysed, seeing his image in

15

the mirrors of her eyes as she stooped over him.

His image and the laser she held and the gout of searing heat which turned the universe into an all-engulfing darkness.

2

He wandered in a darkness shot with blobs and patches of illumination; brilliantly glowing areas like individual rooms each holding a fragment of memory, each tinged with its own emotion. A parade through hate and fear and pain and joy. One he had taken too often so that now the rooms had become hatefully familiar; the events he relived the scars of aching wounds.

Taylor. Quimper. Finch. Carter. Cole and Machen who had turned into things of horror. Ovidio smeared like paint over the hull in a grotesque travesty of a man. Stacy who drank. Lydon who dealt in ghosts. Asner. Owen. Noventes. Erica with her eyes and lips and her gift of love.

Varl twisted, muttering, locked in recurrent nightmare. Seeing again those he had led to their deaths, the faces that accused or screamed or pleaded with empty, weeping eyes. Knowing failure again, the pain of loss, the last dreadful period when his mind had seemed to burn within his skull and his tormented body had jerked and convulsed to the impact of destructive energies.

Waking he looked at a ghost.

'Erica!' He reared, hands outstretched, reaching for the woman standing beside the bed on which he lay. A tall, blonde woman dressed in a plain garment that covered her from neck to mid-thigh, from shoulder to wrist. 'Erica!'

She was warm and active and he buried his face in the warm softness between her breasts as his hungry hands roved over the figure he had known so well. A caress that was more than a desire to touch. One intended to hold, to grip, to reassure, to never, ever relinquish.

'My darling!' His voice was a betrayal of his need. 'You came back to me. You came back!'

'No!' He heard a snap and felt the sting of acrid vapours in his nostrils. Gas from the ampoule she held and which sent him back and away, gasping but, suddenly, fully alert. 'This isn't a dream, Kurt. Your woman is where all the dead go.'

'But — '

'I'm not Erica, you fool!' Anger edged her tone. 'I'm Edallia. Edallia Kramer. Just in case you've forgotten we've met before.'

The headdress was gone, the cloak, the silvered eyes. The paint and barbaric adornment but the mouth remained and the body he had touched was one he remembered.

'You put me down,' he said. 'Betrayed me — '

'I saved your life.'

'With a poisoned dart? And what about the laser?'

'They wanted you dead,' she said patiently. 'They had tried you and condemned you and were set on your execution. It wasn't enough for you just to fall. So I used the gun to sear your scalp. They thought I'd burned your brains. The smoke and blood sobered them and no one wanted to look too close.'

And none of them would have wanted to dispose of the body. Shocked, frightened, blasted out of their blood-hunger, they would have run back to their safe, snug, civilised lives. The woman would have had a free hand.

'I manage.'

'Sure.' Beneath her garment the mounds of her breasts moved with liquid grace as she shrugged, 'We all manage. Now get up and get busy. I'll be in the salon.'

'Wait!' He rose as she halted at the door. 'Why?' he demanded. 'Why do it?'

'Because you're Captain Kurt Varl.'

'That's reason enough?'

'For me, yes,' she said. 'That's reason enough.'

She left and he turned to the washbowl and faucet set against the wall of the cabin. A mirror was set above it and he assessed his damages as he assessed his situation. He was on board a vessel, that was obvious, a ship of a small class that even now was hurtling through space. The cabin told him that and the unmistakable quiver transmitted by the hydee field. The reason why she had saved him and was taking him somewhere could wait. Other things could not.

The dagger that had torn his cheek had

left a gash over an inch long and the blood seeping from the wound had dried to mask his face with a brownish film. More dried blood had matted his hair from the shallow wound on his scalp; one seared and blackened from the fury of the laser. A neat shot; an inch to one side and he would be dead. As it was the bone had remained untouched but the ache was something he could do without.

Varl studied her from where he lay on the bed. The blonde hair was cut short to form a helmet framing her skull, the face which showed a hardness hitherto masked by the paint she had worn. The eyes, devoid now of silver and mirrored contact lenses, were a hard and vibrant blue. The mouth, while still wide and full, was firm, the lips compressed now as if she tasted something bad.

'Finished?'

He said, not moving his stare, 'You remind me of someone.'

'I know, Erica. But we aren't the same.' She added, more gently, 'She's dead, Kurt. Staring at me won't make her come back. Nothing will do that.'

21

'You don't have to tell me.'

'No.' She became brusque again. 'You're a mess. Better clean up before you eat.'

'After you've explained something. Why take me to the party if you intended to save me?'

'They wanted you dead,' she said. 'They wouldn't have rested until you were. On Ceruti or some other world they'd have arranged it. The only way to make you safe from them was to fake your end. Now they can sleep at night.'

'And you?'

'I sleep well enough.' Her lips quirked, softened a little. 'That's more than you can say.'

It eased as he washed away the mess, rinsing his mouth and letting a cold stream numb his cheek and scalp. A dispenser provided dressings and he sealed both wounds with a flexible, transparent film. Dried blood stained his blouse, the smears falling from the material as he held it beneath the faucet. Washed, clean, he looked twice the man who had risen from the bed.

In the salon Edallia was waiting.

Varl strode towards her, pausing as he neared her table, eyes narrowing as he recognised her companion. Normal clothing made him look smaller but there was no mistaking his bulk, the rich sheen of his ebony skin.

Sabatova lifted a hand. 'Peace, brother. We're on the same side.'

His words were slurred, his jaw swollen, eyes reddened with recent pain. Before him on the table stood a bowl that had contained soup — now empty. A phial of tablets lay beside it and he swallowed a couple as Edallia waved a hand in introduction.

'Meet Ian, Kurt. My backup.'

'He tried to kill me.'

'He tried to save you,' she corrected. 'Knock you out and pretend to strangle you. Instead you got in first. You could have broken his neck.'

And would have done if the man hadn't been so strong. Varl watched as he rose from the table, a little stiffly, but he seemed to bear no animosity. The touch of his hand was firm, cool, and his smile was genuine.

'I misjudged you,' he said. 'I was there to stop you getting hurt but I was the one who took the bruises. Well, it happens. The next time I'll be more careful.' To Edallia he said, 'Watch yourself. This man is a killer.'

'I know that. Thirty times over.'

'That talk is for fools,' Sabatova was curt. 'For those idiots back on Ceruti. I saw his face when he attacked me. I read his eyes. There aren't many like him now. Be warned.'

Varl took his seat as the giant walked away, saying nothing as a waitress cleared the table, setting a dish of various morsels before him. The salon was half-full, the tables occupied with a score of men and women, most of middle-age, some young, a few old. The usual types to be found on most vessels plying between the worlds. Among them Edallia was a goddess of some ancient time.

'There's no one here to be afraid of,' she said. 'You can relax.'

'What makes you say that?'

'I was watching your eyes. You've checked every person in the room. A habit?'

He shrugged and helped himself to a scrap of pastry dusted with spice and filled with a sweet combination of pulverised fruit. She followed his example, holding the morsel between her teeth, savouring it as she studied him. A big man, hard, his face like that of a pagan idol. A killer as Sabatova had said and not only in the line of duty. She watched as he ate, aware that every other woman in the salon was doing the same, as every man had looked at her. The penalty of being different in more ways than one. The superficial appearance was nothing; it was what lay beneath which made a person stand above the crowd.

She said, 'Something is bothering me. You let yourself be picked up by a stranger in a street. Why?'

'You were a beautiful stranger.'

'That's no answer.'

Varl selected another morsel, bit into it, leaned back as the waitress came to add another dish to the first. One filled with succulent meats, thin pancakes, a rich sauce and three kinds of vegetables. A pot of tisane accompanied it and he poured, sniffing at the herbal odour, tasting it before emptying the cup.

'Kurt?'

'I had the impression I was being followed,' he said. 'Of being ushered into a trap. I was safer with company than without.'

'The hovercar,' she said. 'I saw it.'

'One that had stopped without apparent reason. Another could have been ahead.'

'And you figured if I was bait it was better to walk into the trap than be carried.' She reached for the tisane and filled her cup. Stood thinking. 'Who did you think was after you?'

'Don't you know?'

'Would I ask if I did?'

'Yes,' he said. 'I think you would. Let's just say I was wary of your friends.'

'They weren't my friends. I joined them for a reason.' She sipped at her tisane. 'We're sparring. Fencing. Wasting time. From where I sit it's a game you don't like playing. My guess is you were following a hunch. Another habit?'

'Maybe.'

'Habits are things to get rid of. They

can be like markers. Most men who want to hide are found because of their habits. Know what I mean?'

'A man likes blondes, walks to the right, wears bright colours, sleeps with the windows open, sits with his back against a wall. Habits. What are yours?'

Varl concentrated on the meal when she didn't answer, chewing the meat well before swallowing, barely touching the pancakes, ignoring the sauce. When he'd finished the dish was still half-full. The tisane had grown cold and he signalled for more. After the waitress had left he stared at the woman.

'You're right about one thing — I don't like wasting time. So how about some straight answers? Where is this ship heading?'

'Pikadov.'

'And?'

'Then I take you to — '

Varl snapped, harshly, 'Forget it! You're not taking me anywhere — '

'As you say.' Her smile held no humour. 'Let me put it another way. After Pikadov I escort you — if you agree — to another world to see a friend of yours. An old friend.'

'Why?'

'He wants to see you.'

'Why do you bother? Orders? Pay?' He added at her nod, 'How much?'

'That's my business, but it's enough.'

'And if you can't deliver?' He answered his own question. 'You get nothing. A contingent fee — only a fool would employ you on any other basis. Well, if you hope to collect, you'll quit dodging the point. Who and where?'

For a moment she hesitated then, meeting his eyes, said, 'Earth, Polar North. Your friend is Nasir Kalif.'

An old friend — Edallia had revealed an ironic sense of humour. The Comptroller of Earth Confederation was certainly far from young. But a friend?

'Forget it.' Varl rose from the table, 'I'm not interested.'

'He said you'd feel like that.' She rose in turn to stand close to him. 'But he told me to tell you something. Not just that he needs you, that he does, but that there's a chance for you to get even. He said you'd understand what he meant. Do you?' She saw the sudden change of his face, the naked animal peering through his eyes and knew a sudden fear. 'Kurt? Kurt, is anything wrong?'

'No.' He took a deep, shuddering breath. 'I'm fine.'

'And you'll come with me?' She smiled with genuine pleasure as he nodded. 'Good. Let's drink to that.'

She reached for the tisane, sipped, spat the liquid back into the cup. 'To hell with this stuff. It lacks guts. Come to my cabin and let's seal the bargain in real liquor.' Then meaningfully, she added, 'The journey will last days yet — and you've still to enjoy your prize.'

3

When young Nasir Kalif had studied history, seeking the facts behind the rise and fall of empires, the fragmentation of seemingly invulnerable societies. Studies which he had used to climb his way to power until now he directed the destinies of all the worlds comprising Earth Confederation. A high position and one it had taken a long time to reach. One he could hold only as long as he demonstrated his ability to maintain the even flow of trade and traffic between the worlds. At times it was hard.

'Sir?' The voice came from a speaker. 'Are you awake?'

For a moment he was tempted to remain silent then, recognising the childish stupidity of such a move, he touched the button that lifted the back of his couch to leave him sitting upright in bed.

'Sir?'

'I'm awake.' His voice sounded cracked

and he took a deep breath and swallowed and spoke again. 'You may come in, Captain. Bring me some brandy.'

An odd drink for a man just woken from a shallow sleep but position held advantages and if he had learned nothing else in his long, long life he had learned to enjoy small pleasures. The comfort of a soft bed, brandy when he wanted it, tea, spiced cakes, warm baths.

He stretched in the scented water, not looking at his body; the emaciated frame ruled by stringent diets. The chest with the livid scar, which showed where the mechanical heart that kept him alive, had been inserted. The other marks of surgical skill which, to date, had doubled the once-accepted life span of three score and ten years.

Lifted from the bath, dried, dressed, sitting with tea and a second brandy, he went through the familiar ritual to gather and direct his strength. A discipline of the mind preceding a frugal breakfast. Only then was he ready for the business of the day.

Until noon it was routine then he said,

'Prepare the recording.'

'Yes, sir.' His personal aide had remained in his quarters. Major Brusac had higher rank and a broader awareness of his responsibilities. 'The visitors?'

'Show them in.'

Varl advanced as he'd anticipated, striding with unconscious arrogance over the tesselated floor to where the Comptroller sat in his throne-like chair. Edallia, accompanying him, stayed discretely to one side.

'It's good to see you again, Kurt.'

'The pleasure isn't mutual.'

'Mine is genuine though our parting was abrupt.' To the woman Kalif said, 'Take a chair. Be patient. Major?'

'Sir!'

'Begin.'

The hall was large, sombre in diffused lighting, a darkness that deepened as the major operated a control. The tesselated floor became the focus of shadows, thick, swirling, then, suddenly, becoming alive with light and movement.

Watching, Varl sucked in his breath.

Before his eyes a devil was dancing. A

multi-legged horror with feet of lavender flame that exploded buildings into flying rubble, gouged craters in the streets, pulped the tiny motes of running figures into smears of blood and bone. Savage destruction accompanied by a shrilling, high-pitched whine; sound which drowned out the roar of collapsing buildings, the screams of the hurt and dying.

It terminated as Kalif lifted a hand, his voice calm, detached over the continuing scene of carnage.

'This happened on Lzicar. A courier arrived with a cargo of mail seconds before it began. He was both lucky and intelligent. He activated his emergency recorder and waited to gain what information he could. Unfortunately he waited too long.'

Edallia said, 'Dead?'

'His ship crushed and him with it. The recorder was sealed and the tape managed to survive. The technicians have worked on it, naturally, but what you see is what actually happened.'

Fragments pieced together to form a whole and that whole forming a monument to a man who no longer existed. An ordinary, hard-working cog in the complex of worlds forming his environment. Taking mail from one to another, his ship travelling far faster than the speed of light. Beating all radio communication yet discovered. A modern mailman — there were a million like him.

Varl hunched forward, watching, light from the holograph touching his face. Accentuating the planes and hollows, the pits that held his eyes. His hands, resting on his knees, quivered a little; a muscular reaction accompanied by a small jerking at the corner of his mouth.

'Soon,' whispered Kalif. 'I think — now!'

The recording jumped, flickered, steadied to show a vista of purple clouds against an emerald sky. In the far distance the loom of mountains shone with golden glitters as sunlight reflected from eternal glaciers. A scene of peace against which the hovering vessel presented an image of nightmare; vaned, spined, set in bizarre configurations. The creator of the beast that ravaged the town.

A bad analogy and he knew it; one too loaded with emotive elements that could hamper the cold process of logical deduction. The ship was just a ship. The lavender flames the focal point of destructive beams. The attack itself no worse than others that had occurred too often during Earth's history. The Vikings had done as much. The Gauls. The hordes of Ghengis Khan. Developed technology had deepened the horror and yet, basically, all had remained the same. A man could be killed only once and whether by stone axe or sword or bullet or bomb the end result was the same,

Blood, guts, skin, bone — the erasure of a personal universe.

'Again.' Varl's voice was a nail grating across slate. 'Play it again.'

'Later. Now we — '

'I want to see that ship. Play it again.'

The beams flared into life again, the buildings fell apart, the running crowds were wiped out as if they had been ants beneath a blowtorch and then the jerking, the loom of mountains, the vessel framed against them.

'Freeze it!' Varl didn't move as he snapped the order. 'Bring it up!'

It grew as he watched, swelling beneath the adjustment of the lasers, steadying and remaining steady aside from a ripple-effect impossible to eradicate because of damage. A sight he would never forget. One he had seen before.

And it was with him again. The fragment of nightmare that refused to die; running now like a recording of its own.

Space, himself crouched at a gun, the alien ship before him. A voice in his ears.

'All ready, Kurt.'

Ready as he was ready and, as the blazing shape of the vessel touched the curve of the *Odile* a bow, he jammed back the release. Holding the gun steady as laser fire reached to hit and blossom into green sparkles. Ending the attack before the alien could move.

'Now, girl! Now!'

The flare of torpedoes and a sun blossomed where the ship had been.

Varl groaned, feeling again the impact of blasting radiation that tore him from the gun and sent him to the full extent of his line. To swing him behind the protection of the *Odile* now crawling with green and lavender fire, shimmering with a golden brightness that died to leave a darkened hull.

A vessel that had become a tomb.

He had torn his way into it, raced through it to the control room, slowing as he saw the sheen of golden hair. Erica, still at her position and, please God, still alive. A prayer uttered too late. A thing he had known as he reached her, turned her towards him, saw the face, the ravaged flesh, the dead, empty eyes.

'The rescue ship found you lying at her feet,' said Kalif as if he had read Varl's mind. 'Moaning, twitching, knees drawn up in the foetal position. Dying from the radiant energy that had destroyed the ship and everything living inside it. They took you, put you in an amniotic tank, carried you to where the best treatment known could be provided. They washed your body with a continuous flow of fresh blood. Used isotopes to nullify the radioactive particles triggering your synapses. Cleansed your bones, your brain. They did it at my order. You owe me your life.'

'You expect me to be grateful?'

'I expect to be paid.' Kalif gestured and the recording died. 'Twenty-seven thousand men, women and children died in that city. Another fifteen were injured, a high proportion seriously. Half of the residential section is ruins. Most of the industry is gone. The factories, warehouses, processing plants — need I describe it all in detail?'

'No.'

'Then I'll get to the point. You saw it happen. It's happened before. Why?'

Varl said, 'Before? This isn't the first time?'

'Three other towns on three different worlds have all suffered similar attack. In those cases there were no survivors. On Lzicar we were lucky. They must have thought the courier a threat of some kind. They blasted his ship and vanished. 'But why did they attack at all?'

'I don't know.'

'An honest answer.' Kalif was patient. 'Give me an intelligent guess.'

'Not for food because they destroyed the warehouses. Not for accommodation because they destroyed the buildings. Not for slaves because they killed them all. The same goes for loot — raiders don't pick it out of rubble.'

'Which leaves?'

'Two possibilities,' said Varl. 'They just wanted to smash things flat or they were testing the defences.'

'There weren't any.'

'They couldn't know that. The only way to be sure was to invite return fire. Remember they ran when the courier arrived. It was another vessel, a potential source of danger, so they hit and run.'

'Cowards,' said Edallia, 'is that what they are?'

'Is that what you'd call a forward patrol?' Varl looked at her. 'They go out, contact the enemy then return to report. There are easier ways to make a living.' To the Comptroller he said, 'How are you going to stop them?'

'I don't know. I want you to tell me.'

'Equip ships with guns. Arm the towns. Keep up a continuous patrol.'

'Go after them,' said Edallia. 'Hit them where it hurts.'

'That's been tried,' said Kalif. 'Five

ships so far each with a full compliment of officers and men. Four are still on operational duty. The other didn't report back to base. It went out and it didn't come back. My guess is it didn't know how to get where it wanted to go. None of them do. You could tell them, Kurt.'

'You've got all I can give.'

'No. The details, yes, the account of what happened, the fate of those who rode with you in the *Odile*. You raved about that often enough when in the amniotic tank. More when you were out of it and being questioned by the medical technicians who struggled to save your life and sanity. But details aren't enough,' Kalif gestured to his aide and, as the recording began again, silent but no less horrible, he said, 'Look at it, Kurt. It's your own kind that's being destroyed. As the *Odile* was destroyed. As Erica.'

Edallia said, 'He's talking of the blood-price, Kurt. Of the duty you owe to the living in return for their dead.'

'Shut up!'

'Did I say I agreed with him?'

Varl rose and stood looking down at

the Comptroller sitting like an ancient mummy in his chair. Light from the holograph touched his face with shifting colours as the ship swelled in the projection its fury emulating the anger building within him.

An anger Kalif ignored.

'You ran,' he said quietly. 'The memories hurt too much. They sent you running from the hospital where you had been made whole again. But they travelled with you. All of them. Ghosts you couldn't put to rest. But now — those ghosts have become real.' His hand lifted to gesture at the recording. 'You've seen a ship like that before. You know where it came from. You know how it found our universe. How many towns have to be destroyed before you accept what has to be done? How many worlds?'

'To hell with that!' Varl snarled his anger, 'What are those towns to me? Those worlds? I'll get the bastards but for reasons of my own and, by God, you'll pay for it!'

4

Polar North was a city sunken beneath the ice. One containing workshops, barracks, laboratories, gymnasiums, a crematorium, a garden. One containing the statue of a man.

Staring at it Edallia Kramer felt awe.

Not because of its size, though it was too large to take in at a glance, but in the expression of the face. It was up-tilted a little, the eyes open as if staring into the glory of the beyond. The eyes of a man transformed. One who had found the key that had released the locks binding Mankind to one small world.

'Ludwig Kreutzal,' said the Comptroller. 'In my opinion the most important man of our race.'

'That could be argued.'

'And often is,' he agreed. 'Some think the laurel should go to one of those who beat back the frontiers of disease; Pasteur, Lister, Erlich, Semmelweis — the list is

42

long. Others talk of Marconi, Volta, Rutherford, but Ludwig Kreutzal did something no one had ever done before. His discovery was unique to himself and not built on the foundations laid by others. Other men have given us extended life, an erasing of the burden of labour, electronic wizardry. Kreutzal gave us the stars.'

The hyper drive which broke the chains of the Einstein restriction on speeds faster than light. The hydee that had given the universe to mankind and with it a host of troubles. Many had been resolved. Some would linger. Always there would be more and, always, the fear remained that, one day, something would be met which would prove too big for solution.

Nasir Kalif shivered at the thought of it.

'Cold?' Edallia glanced at where he stood wrapped in a quilted robe. She, herself, was warm from the beamed heat which followed them along the paths set with crystalline blooms; frost-flowers like gems culled from a hundred different worlds and set among a plethora of delicate fronds and lichens in a host of startling hues. 'We can go back if you want. I've seen enough.'

Kalif ignored her, lingering before the statue as if he were an old-time worshipper at a shrine. But, for him, Kreutzal had been more than a saint even thought he might well have been touched by God. Gone he remained an enigma. Three hundred years ago he had simply vanished on a trial flight of his personal vessel. All logic pointed to the fact that he must have died, certainly be now dead, but stubbornly Kalif clung to the wild hope that, somehow, the genius was still alive. Frozen, perhaps, locked in a form of alien stasis as he drifted in the formless grey region of hyperspace. Or even somewhere beyond where time did not run at the same pace as it did in the universe which had given him birth.

'Comptroller?' Edallia was getting bored. 'Are you finished here?'

He said, without looking at her, 'Think of the universe as a bubble, one surrounded by a thick convoluted skin. Call that skin hyperspace. The hydee throws a ship into it and it travels and, when it emerges, it has beaten the speed of light. Do you understand?'

'Of course.'

'Now think a little further. Suppose we went beyond that skin. Penetrated it. Forced ourselves into another universe — are you with me?'

'Is that what Varl did?'

'Yes. He didn't mean to but that's what happened. He went to combat a menace that threatened commerce and civilisation as we know it. He found an answer but also created a new problem. I'd hoped it wouldn't materialize but it has and must be faced. Varl is our best hope of facing it. What do you think of him?'

She said, 'I saw him fight. I watched as he faced down a roomful of nuts hyped up to kill. He beat them all including the man I'd planted to help him. Poor Ian — well, he'll get over it. And I read his eyes when the dart hit and he tried to get at me. Another foot closer and he'd have cut me to ribbons.'

'What are you saying?'

'Kurt Varl is an animal.'

'All men are that,' he said gently. 'As are all women. Civilisation is based on the ability to master the natural impulses.'

'Restraining the censor,' she said. 'I know what you're getting at. The thalamic block between thought and action. My guess is he hasn't got it.'

'You could be right,' Kalif turned to touch a flower and to study the trace of frost it left on his finger. 'Once he was the master of a ship, trusted, obedient. Then he took the law into his own hands and was made to pay for it. I had a use for the type of man he was and gave him the choice of working for me, for Earth Confederation, or of staying where he was. He chose to work for me and did what had to be done. His reward was to lose everything but his life. I couldn't deny him his freedom so let him escape. Naturally he has been kept under surveillance.'

'Ready to be picked up when you needed him,' Edallia inhaled, inflating her chest, moving her hands over breasts, hips and buttocks. 'Am I so like Erica?'

'Basically, yes.'

'Which is why you gave me the job. Bait to snare your victim.' Her laughter sent chiming tinkles from the frost-plants. 'You could have made a mistake. I think you've caught yourself a tiger.'

'I need a tiger — and you will help to tame him.'

Inside the complex it was warm, the very air seeming to quiver with the throb of organised activity. In a small compartment Varl was studying destruction.

He leaned forward in his chair, staring at the table before him, the scaled-down projection of the recording of the damage done on Lzicar. It was soundless, the flares of lavender throwing spurts of brilliance to highlight his face. Glows that died as Edallia entered to be replaced with a softer illumination from panels set in the ceiling.

'Learn anything?'

'Verification.' His hand gestured at the table, the recorder set beside it. His voice emerged as he touched a button, died as she killed the machine.

'You tell me.'

'The destruction follows a pattern and

47

bears out my guess that the ship was more interested in testing out any defences than the winning of loot. It started with the demolition of all large structures beginning with those with domed roofs. The observatory, a library with a rotunda, a meeting hall, a community centre. Then it moved on to destroy warehouses, industrial plants and other large buildings. A shopping mall, for example. Then the beams lashed out at apparent random.'

'Vicious children playing with dangerous toys?'

'Or frightened men playing it safe.'

'You think that?'

'It could be a combination of the two — but we can't be sure those operating the ship are men.'

'Aliens aren't all that rare. We've bumped into them before.'

'And fought with them,' he agreed. 'Mistakes we never want to repeat. Civilised creatures, no matter how they walk or fly or crawl or look are still that — civilised creatures. But this is the work of barbarians. No, worse than that. Even a barbarian has a reason for wanton destruction.'

'What we saw wasn't necessarily wanton,' she pointed out. 'You said so. It must have been a test.'

'One following others?' Varl shrugged and touched a control. The lights dimmed, the projection flared again in three-dimensional brilliance, this time showing the alien bulk of the bizarre vessel. 'Watch.'

Edallia obeyed, seeing nothing but the ship, the flare of beams.

'So?'

'The last time I saw a ship like that it was more cautious. It had a defensive screen of green fire and could only use its weaponry after the screen had been dropped. It couldn't fire through it,' he explained. 'When it did fire it was, for a second or so, vulnerable.'

She said, again, 'So?'

'No green fire.' He pointed at the vessel now frozen in the holograph. 'It's firing but in bursts. Between them it isn't bothering to protect itself.' He adjusted the magnification. 'Which means it either has grown confident there is no danger from below or it has developed a more efficient system.'

'Coordinated pulses,' she suggested. 'The screen drops when a weapon is fired. A computer link would make it easy.'

'I doubt it.'

'Why?'

'You're the alien commander,' he said. 'Engaged with an enemy ship. You keep firing, but torpedoes are coming at you and you want to be safe. So you order a ceasefire and that takes time. And some hot-headed fool just can't resist an easy target — and that leaves you defenceless.'

'I see.' Her white teeth gnawed thoughtfully at the fullness of her bottom lip. 'But it still could be done.'

'But not with a simple link,' Varl adjusted another control and grunted. 'There! See it?'

A flash of green as the image tilted to fall away into darkness. A hint of colour almost lost in the sudden blurring of the holograph. The last image registered by the camera the courier had used. One taken when he was dead, his ship crushed and sent to scatter itself over the terrain.

'So they have a screen,' said Edallia. 'But you knew that.' She stepped back as he rose from the table, 'What now?'

'The neurological laboratory. They're running some tests.'

One of the technicians had short, dark hair, a pouting mouth, brown eyes and a figure that looked good even in the trim greens she wore off duty. Now, smiling, she stepped towards the man seated in the control-chair. He was big, young, hair a tight mass of crinkled wool over a rounded skull. He was naked to the waist.

'Relax,' she said. 'There's no need for you to get uptight over this. It's routine procedure. Think of it as a way to test your reflex-speed. Comfortable? Good.' She lifted a tray and set it on a stand before him. On it was an upturned glass. Inside the glass was a spider. 'This is a funnel-web spider from Australia,' she explained. 'Its bite is lethal. Once the venom gets into the blood there is no hope of survival. You understand? Now I'm going to remove the glass.'

51

'No! Wait! I — '

'Remember, if it bites you, you are dead.'

The glass lifted, remaining in her hand as she backed away and, on the tray the spider moved a little, turning, freezing as it faced the man in the chair. Long moments during which he sat as if paralysed, eyes bulging, sweat sheening his face and body. Then, as the creature sprang, he swiped at the air, throwing himself down and to one side, rolling on the floor almost frantic with terror.

'All right.' The technician trod on something that crunched. 'It's all over. You're safe now. Get up, get dressed and get back on duty. You'll be notified as to the result.'

'A wipe-out.' An older woman had joined Varl and Edallia; one with white, close-cut hair. The name on her tag was Doctor Muriel Brice. 'Another failure — we get a lot of them.' To the young technician she said, 'You'd better quit now. Have Susan take over.'

'I can manage.'

'Do as I say.' The doctor looked at Varl

52

and shrugged. 'They get to like it too much,' she explained. 'Watching a man sweat, smelling his fear, recognising his weakness. It can affect them and alter their personality.'

'Is that bad?' Edallia frowned as she looked at the chair, the tray, the glass lying on it. 'She must have guts to face those things.'

'The spider isn't real. A model moved with magnets and air. Killing it was just pretence.'

'Then what's the point?' Edallia answered her own question. 'You're trying to discover if those tested have any phobias. A lot of people are scared of arachnids and other forms of life. You're weeding them out, right?'

'That's a part of it but not all. It goes deeper than that.' To the new technician she said, 'Bring in the next one.'

He was slim, pale, as nervous as the other. He licked his lips as the technician explained and tensed as she lifted the glass. Long moments spent in indecision then, in obvious panic, his hand reached out to smash down on the fake spider.

'Better,' said the doctor after he'd gone. 'But not good enough.'

'He killed it,' said Edallia. 'What more do you want?'

'Speed.' Varl was abrupt. 'He waited too long and even then wasn't sure he was doing the right thing. Fear drove him, not instinct. The kind of men we need don't waste time on thought. Most are reluctant to become involved. They are afraid of getting hurt or running foul of the law or breaking custom or earning the disapproval of their kind. Things that slow them down. In a fight there are no rules. No laws. No decency. When a man fights he should fight to kill.'

Doctor Brice said, 'What you are talking about is a special kind of personality. Basically it is a criminal trait. One devoid of all conscience or sense of responsibility or imagination as to the fate of the victim. One with a total dedication to self. You won't find such people in Polar North.'

'No,' admitted Varl. 'But I'll find them in Hell.'

5

Hell was a place on a raw and lonely world blasted by the savage radiation of triple suns. A fissure gaping wide and deep as if some monstrous axe had chopped at the planet, splitting its crust and magma, leaving a spot which had become a festering sore. One filled with a plethora of voracious life and of interest to those with a taste for the bizarre. A haven for the freaks and failures to be found in any society.

'Freeze!'

The guide was broad, tough, taciturn, one cheek mottled by the brand of an ugly scar. He stepped cautiously ahead, the long pole he carried prodding at the dirt. Something leapt from the loam to wrap itself around the shaft, to move like a greased snake towards the gloved hands of the guide. A snake that reared with a rasp of scales as blue fire sprang from metal conductors to send it in a twitching heap to the dirt.

'Walk steady now,' he said. 'And bear to the right.'

The left-hand path was wider, flanked by a tall bush dotted with brilliant flowers. As Edallia hesitated a small animal lunged from the undergrowth and darted along it. Halfway down it sprang high into the air as thin, vicious hisses echoed from the bush. Falling, it revealed the spines that had impaled it.

'A harpoon tree,' said the guide. 'Easy enough to avoid if you keep your eyes open. Of course the crabants like to lurk on the other side and you've always got to remember what can drop from above.'

Insects as large as cats and dogs, nooses from trailing vines, searing acids tipped from brimming pods, spores blasted in a parasitical rain. Hell was well-named.

Its inhabitants maintained its reputation.

'This is the deadline,' said the guide. 'Keep to the middle of the path and you won't have too much trouble. They manage to keep it relatively clear. Once you reach the village, well, that's another matter.' He looked from one to the other;

Varl, Edallia, the black giant Sabatova, a handful of others. 'No one can help you once you cross the line,' he warned. 'We keep order outside because of the tourists but that's all. The rest we leave alone.'

To fight and live and die in their own way. The universe was too large and worlds too plentiful for bureaucrats to have their way. And the memory of the horror of the Debacle would stop any who had thoughts of grandeur. Earth had been devastated when the oppressed billions had risen to throw off the yoke of their masters.

'This way,' Varl took the lead. 'Stay close.'

The path was clear and straight and tempting — so he moved to one side and forced his way past a clump of bushes and around a sloping pit to where a ridge ran alongside the cleared way. A less easy journey and twice he had to kill things which took a sudden interest and three times he paused to throw dirt at a seemingly innocent plant to have it turn into something else.

'A balanced ecology,' grumbled Sabatova. 'And we are upsetting the balance.' He tripped and almost fell and grunted as he tested his ankle. This was no time or place to break a leg. Ahead Varl turned, impatient at the delay.

'Keep moving!' he snapped. 'If you can't keep up then return to the hostel.'

A temptation; the place was air-conditioned, guarded, filled with comforts for the benefit of tourists. But to return was to admit defeat and, maybe, to face Varl's anger.

Sabatova kept moving.

Along the ridge to a levelled place set beneath a surround of trees. One backed by the side of the fissure, the area scraped clean of vegetation. To a jumble of buildings made of local timber, sod, tamped dirt, gathered stone. A place of bowed walls and sagging roofs with porches floored with stained coverings all covered in a wild profusion of exotic fungi, moulds, lichens, slimes.

'Welcome!' A man came to greet them. Tall, wearing black touched with silver, his hair shaped to frame a narrow, pointed face. His eyes held madness. 'It is good to meet new arrivals. Those bearing gifts as tribute and one who is most certainly beyond price.' A hand lifted towards Edallia. 'Come, my dear, I have need of a new consort. In an hour you will be my queen.'

She said, flatly, 'Go to hell!'

'Hell? We are there already.' His laughter rose, thin, grating, 'Hell is our home.'

And home was hell in more ways than one. Varl looked at a scatter of men moving slowly over the clearing; thin, skeletal, dressed only in rotting leaves with crude tools in their hands with which they scraped the dirt.

'Scum,' said the man in black. 'Debtors who couldn't pay. Others who lacked the guts to carry out what they tried. There's no law in Hell but there are penalties.'

'So much for freedom,' said Sabatova.

'It's here if you want it.' A black-clad arm lifted to wave a hand at the cliffs to either side, the rock coated with thick vegetation. 'No law. No regulations. No police. Do what you like and go where you like. Live as you please until you run into someone who doesn't like your style.

Some shoot it out. Some compromise. A few build empires.'

'Like you?'

'You may call me Dobkin. I do not insist on a title and there is no need for you to kneel.'

Sabatova shook his head as he looked at the others.

'He's crazy.'

Lost in a make-believe world induced by the drugs contained in the riot of fungi. Hallucinogens that had converted reality so that, for him, the clearing was the broad acres of his domain, the visitors those coming to shower him with gifts as they paid tribute to his majesty.

'A harmless fool,' said Edallia. 'Forget him.'

A mistake; Dobkin might act the fool but he was far from harmless. For now it was safer to cater to his illusion.

Varl said, 'Your majesty I come seeking your aid. I need strong men, fighters, champions to back my cause. For them will be riches and the loot of worlds. For you — ' He broke off, shrugging. 'What can I give to one who has everything?'

'The woman. Give me the woman.'

'She is yours — when I have the men.'

'You defy me?' Anger convulsed the narrow face and a hand lifted to pluck at the collar of the silver-edged tunic. A moment of strain then, with an abrupt change of mood, the hand dropped, the anger turning into a smile. 'You are bold and I like that. And you recognise my standing which is gratifying. Come, let me escort you to my palace.'

It was little better than the rest of the buildings, the walls of stone, the porch set with chairs in which sat a motley collection of men. They watched with hard, calculating suspicion as Varl and the others approached. One was naked to the waist and seemed to be elaborately tattooed then Varl realised he was contaminated with some alien growth which had taken root in his flesh.

'I'm Knowles,' he said. 'Have you medicines? Drugs? Something to rid me of this damned parasite?'

'Use acid. Burn it free.'

'I can't. It's sunk too deep.'

'Too bad.' Varl saw the eyes of the

others watching him, the glint of mirth they contained. 'Maybe it isn't a parasite at all,' he suggested. 'My guess is you've got yourself a symbiote. Does it give you pleasant dreams?'

'He's got you there, Knowles.' A man beat his hand on the arm of his chair. 'We've all heard you calling to your little Matilda. A hell of a name to give a mould. Matilda.'

'Smart,' said another as the laughter died away. 'You read him right, mister.' He rose to stand before Varl. 'I'm Bilton. Dobkin's right hand, you might say. We get along and so do others who join us if they're willing to share.' His eyes moved towards Edallia. 'Maybe you're our kind. At least you knew enough to dodge the trap we set on the path. You want to join up with us?'

'Just you? The ones I see?'

'We've got a few women and there's a few more out in the brush. Well?'

Varl looked at the shabby buildings, the dirt and squalour, the men sitting around, the watching shape of the pretend-king.

'No.'

'You figure you're too good for us?' Bilton stepped closer, eyes angry, voice thickening with rage. A man doped and trembling on the edge of violence. 'Come to see the animals, is that it? Come to laugh. By God, I'll see you laugh before I'm through with you. I'll have you begging for a quick end.' His hand moved, steel flashing as he lifted the knife. 'I'll teach you to — ' He broke off, looking at the charred hole in his chest, the blood spurting from his heart. At the laser in Varl's hand. 'You bastard! You — '

'Hold it!' Varl spun, the weapon covering the others as Bilton fell. 'Ian! Watch my back! The rest of you cover the village. If anything moves start firing and don't hesitate.'

'You killed him.' Shock had snapped the pretend-king from his fantasy. 'Shot him down like a dog.'

'He talked too much.' Varl was cold, 'And he had a knife. I don't let scum like that threaten me. Remember that. All of you. Now give me some answers. Are you all there are or is there another village or town or whatever? Come on, damn you, talk!' The laser burned holes in the floor, sent clumps of fungi rising in acrid smoke. 'Talk!'

There was a town set deep in the fissure. A bizarre place of a confusion of architectural styles roofed in odd and peculiar ways. The streets were mostly of tamped dirt interspersed with paved areas. Windows were small, set high, closely barred. The doors belonged to fortresses. A dog eat dog society in which each made his own way. One in which Varl knew his way around.

'You're good,' said Mulcaster. 'Word came down from the village about how you handled yourself but that means little. You're what? Seven men and a woman against the rest of us. Just how far do you reckon to get?'

He sat in a pool of steaming hot water fed from a mineral spring. A plump man, no longer young, his face seamed and creased with lines of hard-won experience. Sparse hair was scraped over the top of a balding skull. A man who had lived in Hell for most of his life and had mastered his environment. Varl had known such men must exist. He had spent three hours deciding the best to approach, another five arranging the interview.

'I'll go as far as I want to,' he said. 'Eight people, united, can stand against a mob. Especially when they've no choice.'

'You selling your power?'

'No.' Varl stretched in the water luxuriating in its warmth. The pool was neutral ground and he was safe. 'I came to collect a crew. Hard men who can face danger. Those with combat experience and accustomed to space. They must be willing to fight and kill.'

'And die?'

'No. I want no potential suicides. It'll be my neck too. But I don't want cowards for the same reason.'

Mulcaster said, 'Most have a reason for coming to Hell and a better one for staying here.'

'I can offer good pay and amnesty for any crimes they might have committed. That holds even if they don't make the final grade. It's a fair offer.'

'Backed by whom?' Mulcaster pursed

his lips as Varl told him. 'Earth Confederation, eh? Haven't they men of their own?'

'Not the kind I'm looking for.' Varl moved his arm through the water. 'I've things you need and can arrange more to be delivered. Find me the right kind of men and we can make a deal. If you aren't interested I'll find someone who is.'

'Such as?'

'Karpov, maybe.' Varl watched Mulcaster's eyes. 'Hannes. Or there's always Burdis. He might be even less greedy than you are. Maybe he's got a bath too. I'll see.'

'Wait!' Mulcaster reared to his feet as Varl moved to the edge of the pool. 'I'm interested. How many do you want?'

6

The room held a bed, a chair, a small table backed by a mirror, a cabinet in which could be stored clothes. The floor was bare boards covered with an apology of a carpet. The window was a minute square set with bars and masked by a curtain. There was a single lamp set in a holder beside the door. It was equipped with internal bolts and, outside, a strong hasp and hoop could hold a padlock of the occupier's choice.

A prison in which Edallia fumed.

She strode five paces and reached the window. Turning five more carried her back to the door. A box five paces square with a ceiling eight feet from the floor. One of a row that formed the upper gallery of the lodging house Varl had chosen.

He had hired them all, setting guards at each end of the passage that ran beside them. Men who watched while their companions rested, the rooms given over to them and the equipment they owned. To Edallia he had been curt.

'You're a woman and valuable as a hostage. I don't want to have to buy you back or waste time looking for you. Just stay put until I get back.'

She hadn't argued, smiling as if in full agreement, watching as he went out to taste the excitement of the town and conduct his business. The arrogant bastard! Did he think she couldn't look after herself?

'No!' The guard at the end of the passage was firm as he blocked her way, 'I've my orders — no one is to leave.'

'How are you going to stop me?'

'Please — '

'Surely you wouldn't shoot me?'

She stepped closer towards him, smiling, shoulders thrown back, one thigh sliding over the other as she used the subtle weapons of her sex. 'Demus, isn't it? Cran Demus? Well, Cran, we haven't had much chance to get to know each other as yet, but that can change. All I want is a little air and — ' She lowered her eyes, a woman too embarrassed to go into detail. 'I won't be long. I promise you.'

Then she was past him, moving on down the stairs, to the lower section where a middle-aged woman stared at her before returning to her kneading. On and out into the street to the smells of dust and leaves and baking and washing. To the life and activity of the town.

'Hi, there!' A man smiled and nodded.

'Help you, lady?' An urchin, grimed, ragged, his hand reaching to touch her clothing as he stared up into her face. 'Guide you to the casino? Cerney's House? The freak show? Three dron and I'll take you wherever you want to go.'

'Where is your mother?'

'Dead. Pay me?' His hand was hungry as it trembled before her. 'Three dron — you can afford it.'

'Beat it!' The voice was harsh, softening as the boy scuttled away. 'You're new here, aren't you? May I be of help?'

He was tall, smooth, neatly dressed. The leather of his shoes gleamed against the dirt of the street and his nails were free of grime. A neat, clean, fastidious man with a broad-planed face and a sensuous, mobile mouth. Then she saw his eyes and knew he was an animal shaped like a man.

'My name is Sinden,' he said. 'Eugene Sinden. I heard what the lad suggested but he is young and has yet to learn. What need for a woman like you to trust to luck to make her fortune? Cerney's House?' His shrug was an echo of his disdain, 'A place of assignation where flesh is offered and purchased. That is not for you. Neither is the spectacle of the unfortunate. Not unless your taste lies in that direction?'

A man playing with her, Edallia could sense it, but one who could get played with in turn. A dangerous game and she knew it but an exciting one and the challenge was hard to resist.

She said, smiling, 'I find no pleasure in the deformed but it is important not to be bored. Perhaps you could suggest something which would entertain me?'

'Of course. It will be my pleasure. If you will permit me?' He stepped forward before she could answer, his left hand taking her right, his right hand snatching the laser holstered at her waist. As he pressed the muzzle against her side he said, 'It would be a needless waste to kill you. Just walk at my side and do not struggle.'

'Where are you taking me?'

'That is for me to decide.' His tone hadn't changed nor had his smile and, too late, she realised she had badly underestimated his danger. 'You will obey,' he said. 'You will do everything I order without objection or hesitation.'

'Or you will shoot?' She kept her voice light, tinged with laughter. 'That will be interesting — the gun lacks a charge.'

'I doubt that, but if it becomes necessary we shall put it to the test. Incidentally I am not alone. Attack me or try to run and others will take action.'

A bluff? It was a possibility and she looked to either aide, seeing nothing and gaining hope then, suddenly, she saw the shadow at the mouth of an alley between two buildings, the stance of it, the rifle it held.

A bodyguard; Sinden would have at least one and maybe more. The man lounging beside the lodging house, for example, or the one lower down apparently engrossed with a torn boot. Both would be slow to get into action and she discounted them. Sinden himself, the gun at her side, the man in the shadows.

To press the release of the weapon would take time and would only be done after she had made her move. A part of a second, perhaps, but the very proximity of the gun was in her favour. To move, dodge the beam, to neutralise its threat, to do the same with the man then to deal with the lurking bodyguard.

She stumbled, lowering her head so as to mask the decision in her eyes. The gun moved against her side, the muzzle slipping from her body, turning aside as she grabbed at the barrel, her free hand lifting as she straightened, the fingers hooked, the nails raking at Sinden's eyes.

'Bitch!' He reared back, blood streaming down his ravaged cheeks. 'You bitch!'

The laser lifted in her grasp, firing, the beam catching her blouse, the skin beneath it. A burn which triggered her innate savagery and she threw strength into her hand and arm, using his own against him, turning the muzzle to rest against his stomach as she fought to close his finger on the trigger.

Smoke plumed, drowned in a gush of blood as the beam seared into the soft flesh beneath his chin, burning its way up into the mouth, the palate, the brain above.

As he fell she fired at the lurking shadow.

Three shots then it had gone, running, seeing no profit in avenging the dead. The woman kneading dough glanced at her when Edallia returned to the lodging house. Cran Demus stared with startled eyes.

'You're hurt! By God if — '

'An accident. Say nothing. I've things in my room.'

Water, dressings, salves, a new blouse. The burn was minor and soon treated but the near-miss dampened her exhilaration. She had won — but just. Luck had saved her; without it she would be lying dead in the street where Sinden had fallen. And, if Varl learned what had happened, it would make him think her a fool.

He arrived two hours later, looking into her room where she lay resting on the bed.

'Are you all right?'

'Just tired.' She yawned. 'And bored. Any luck?'

'Mulcaster will cooperate. His men will be ready for selection after we've slept.' He stepped towards the bed, halting as she shook her head. 'No?'

'No, Kurt — for now I sleep alone.'

A big red sun hung in the sky when she woke, its sullen hue tinging the houses with a ruddy glow. One that turned Varl's face into that of a demon as he led the way to the hall in which the men were assembled. They lined up at his order and stood, lax, indifferent, their contempt barely masked. Hatred for authority clothed them like a garment,

'I want men,' snapped Varl. 'Men with guts who are willing to fight for rich rewards. You've been told that. If you're not interested then you shouldn't be here.

I don't like wasting my time. You!' His finger stabbed. 'Experience?'

'I was a courier.' The man was sullen. 'Did a regular run for twelve years then they said I'd raided the mail.'

'You're lying! You'd never be given the chance. Out! You!'

'Wait a minute! I'm no scut to be pushed around!'

'I said to get out!' Varl snarled his anger, 'Move before I drop you!' The gun in his hand was no harder than his eyes. 'Next?'

A man who claimed to be an engineer. Another who said he had handled torpedoes. A third who had no battle experience aside from having killed three men in a brawl. Touts. Pimps. Gamblers. Thieves. More who were equally useless.

To Mulcaster Varl said, 'You're not providing what I asked for.'

'You said — '

'I want men, no scum. Fighters not back-stabbing cowards. If this is the best you can do then forget it.'

'Our deal — '

'Forget that too. Well?'

Others appeared, different, standing straight, confident of their abilities and motivated by more than hate. Most had fought in alien wars and had found it irksome to accept the dictates of peace. Some had been mercenaries. Some pirates, raiders, hit-and-run parasites. Beaten and driven into hiding by organised authority. All had experience in space. Not all were men.

'Sylvia Kiouza.' A dark-haired, well-formed woman met Edallia's eyes. 'Ship-girl on the *Valova*.'

'We don't need ship-girls.'

'Why? Have you enough? How about medical assistants then? I can handle the work of an infirmary.'

'Under battle conditions?'

'Yes.'

'That's easy to say.' Varl stepped forward and stared at the woman. 'Have you seen men with their guts hanging out? Their eyes on their cheeks? Arms burned to stubs? Heard them scream? Pray? Beg for an easy end? Killed them out of mercy?'

Swallowing she said, 'I've seen most

things. The *Valova* was a mercenary.'

'Where operating?'

'The Tamara zone. We — '

'Never mind. Crew?'

'Fifteen.'

'And you were the only ship-girl?'

Varl grunted as she nodded. 'All right. You're in. Next?'

The red sun gave way to the yellow; twin colours burning in conflict before the ruby light fell below the horizon. More men and women appeared, curious, some looking for trouble. One used his boots, tearing open Sabatova's cheek before the giant pounded him unconscious.

The green sun had replaced the yellow by the time they had finished. Back in the lodging house Edallia poured wine.

'Ian?' She handed Sabatova a goblet. 'Kurt?'

Varl drank and stretched and drank again. As Sabatova touched his cheek he said, 'You'd better get that dressed — and thanks.'

'For taking care of that animal? I should have let you shoot it.'

'That would have been a mistake. It's too easy to use a gun. By handling him the way you did you earned the respect of the others.' Varl emptied his goblet and held it out for more wine. 'I guess we've skimmed the cream. We'll give it another sun after we've rested then pull out. We can get them into shape later. If we keep more than half we'll be lucky.'

'They'll stay.' Edallia was confident. 'They're bored and eager for action.'

'But they have to accept discipline. My kind of discipline. And when they know what they're wanted for they may change their minds. What I'm offering is no picnic.'

Sabatov shrugged. 'It's their choice.'

'True.' Varl dismissed the problem. 'Ian, you'd better radio to the depot telling them to expect us. After that get some rest — and don't forget to treat that wound.'

After he'd left Varl lingered and Edallia could sense his tension, his need. One she shared but resisted the temptation to share her bed. But later, when the green sun was being joined by the red, she woke to find him at her side.

He said nothing — nothing needed to be said. It was a matter of basic need and, later, when both were satiated, he slept like a baby at her side.

When she woke he was standing beside her a steaming cup of coffee in his hand.

'Kurt! For me? How nice!' She reared upright, reaching for the cup, the covers falling from her torso to expose her breasts, the wound on her side. She saw the movement of his eyes and felt the need to explain. 'I meant to tell you,' she said. 'It was while — '

'Forget it.' If he knew about Sinden he didn't want to talk about the incident. 'We leave in an hour. There's been a message from Earth.'

'The aliens?'

'Yes.' He was bitter. 'They've hit again.'

7

They struck like destroying angels, bright and beautiful in their glowing hues, terrible in their enigma. The visitations of ancient prophecy come to punish the transgressions of mankind. Burning, smashing, killing, cleansing the loam of its filth. The hand of the Creator rectifying an error.

Fantasy and Nasir Kalif knew it. One that Varl didn't entertain.

He said, 'What happened?'

'We've been hit three times.'

'Details?'

Jason supplied them. He was small, portly, his face normally creased in a smile. Now he was more than serious.

'Two of the towns were small communities of about twenty thousand inhabitants. Both are now rubble. The city of Logis on Tusa is another matter. It is large, about eighty thousand, and growing. The attack commenced at about noon local time. It lasted almost an hour. Casualties are close to thirty thousand dead and seriously injured. Most of the city now lies in ruins. The attack only ended when a patrol ship from the local base arrived on the scene.'

'By accident or luck?'

'Someone radioed for help. It took time to crew the vessel and get it into action.'

Varl nodded. 'Was fire exchanged?'

'Torpedoes were discharged at the alien without any apparent effect.'

'But they drove off the raider.' Wilcox stepped forward from where he had stood at the side of the room. 'A recording was obtained as they made the attack. The projector is ready if you want to see it.'

It was short and somehow unreal. An alien ship poised against an azure sky. Undamaged the tape had retained every detail and Varl narrowed his eyes as the sequence was played. The vessel hanging, moving wreathed in green luminescence as the torpedoes were fired, seeming to vanish as they exploded in gouts of eye-searing brilliance.

As the holograph died he said, 'I want technicians to make a thorough comparison check of both recordings to check the similarity of the ships.'

Kalif nodded. 'I understand. And?'

'A complete rundown of the spectro-scopic pattern of the torpedo-bursts. Maybe we managed to breach their screen. If so we could have vapourised some of their hull and a check might tell us what it's made of.'

'Straws,' said Wilcox. 'You're clutching at straws.'

'You have a better suggestion?' Varl grunted as the man made no reply. To the Comptroller he said, 'Add this to the list. A check on the times of all attacks as far as is known. An extrapolation of flight-paths based on the planets hit and their position in space relative to each other and any common focus. We might be able to find out just where they came from.'

'We know that.'

'I was talking about their emergence-point.' Varl saw the question in Wilcox's eyes, the frown on Jason's forehead. 'Haven't they been briefed?'

'We're aware of your history,' said Jason. 'But how can you find a particular point in limbo?'

'We can't as yet. Maybe we can find a way.'

'But — '

'Why don't you use your brain instead of your mouth?'

Varl snarled his impatience as he paced the floor. A man living on his nerves, over-tense and ready to explode. 'I went into limbo,' he explained. 'All hydee ships do. Something was lurking there. We fought it and the *Odile* went beyond, into another universe — call it U2 for want of a name. We came back and one of the alien vessels followed us. Or was it just one?'

Wilcox, frowning, said, 'I think I understand. If more than one followed you through the barrier then — '

'They could be the raiders. One, two — God knows how many. That's why I want the comparison made. It would help to know if we recorded the same ship twice.'

From where he sat Kalif said, 'Are you suggesting they could have established a base on some galactic world?'

'It's possible. The alternative is that,

somehow, I tore a hole through limbo. If so there's an opening between the two universes. One through which the raiders can come at will. If it exists we must find it.'

'So as to block the raiders, of course.' Jason nodded then added, 'But can you? Block them, I mean?'

Varl shrugged. 'We have to try.'

'And, in the meantime, what?' Jason had his own answer. 'We must protect and guard every city of, say, fifty thousand inhabitants or more. I'm thinking of laser-cannon, self-guided missiles and, for the really large metropolis, squads of patrolling vessels. Once the aliens learn that to attack us is to invite destruction they will leave us alone.'

'To go after the smaller towns instead?' Wilcox shook his head. 'Do you realise the implications of what you are saying?'

Varl was impatient. 'They'll go after the small towns anyway. They've found out what they wanted to know; large cities are defended. All right, it was luck the base was so close and the ship responded so quickly but they don't know that. I don't think you need worry about the big cities — but God help the small.'

And, after them, what?

Kalif could see it as if it were written in letters of fire. Cities would become armed and armoured enclaves with their populations living in fear, forever searching the sky for an alien threat. Human nature would see to that and the natural progression of events. No one would rely on size providing an automatic protection. A modern version of the old walled towns and medieval castles would come into existence; a pattern typical of societies doomed to fall from their own, oppressive weight.

He said, urgently, 'Varl, when will you be ready to leave?'

'When the ship is ready. The crew trained.'

'Ships,' corrected Wilcox. 'You'll be using more than one.'

'I doubt if I'll have a crew for more than one.'

'Volunteers will join you.' He added, hastily, 'Good men, carefully selected. They know what is expected of them.'

'Your men?' Varl thinned his lips as Wilcox nodded. He should have suspected, the man bore the stamp of a uniform, but it made no difference. To the Comptroller he said, 'I want it clearly understood that I am in sole command of the ship I ride in and any that accompany me. My orders must be obeyed without question.'

Wilcox said, 'That is agreeable within certain limits.'

'No limits! I get what I ask for or I walk away from the whole mess. You, your problem, the scum I brought back with me from Hell. Maybe you can use them. If not just drop a bomb on them — Darkside can stand another crater.'

'Take it easy, man!' Watching the contorted face Jason felt a real fear. 'Varl! You'll have what you want. You have our word.'

'Comptroller?'

Kalif said, 'You trusted me once and I didn't let you down. You can trust me again — I swear it.'

'Swearing comes cheap. I want it in writing.'

'Of course. Your command will be signed, sealed and delivered. In the meantime why not drop down to medical for a thorough check? You are still, officially, not discharged from hospitalisation. After that the answers to the questions you asked should be ready.' Kalif added, apologetically, 'I should have told you. I anticipated your requirements.'

As he had done so much else; sensing the nodes of importance, the association between seemingly unrelated incidents. The ability that had lifted him to his present position and would keep him in it while his talent lasted.

When Varl had gone Wilcox released his breath in a long, low susurration.

'Mad,' he said. 'The man is mad.'

'Dangerous, too.' Jason remembered his fear. 'An animal. How can you trust him? A lunatic in charge of a bunch of criminals — why use him at all?'

'Because we have no choice.' Kalif was abrupt. 'He is the only man living who has been to where we have to go. The only one who has had experience of the enemy. He fought an alien ship and destroyed it. What he's done once he can do again.'

Wilcox was bitter. 'So we dance to his tune, eh?'

'Yes.' Kalif met his eyes. 'While we need him we dance to his tune.'

The medical section was sunken deep beneath the polar ice. Varl passed it, moving on to where quiet rooms glowed with the flash of instrument-lights, the air filled with the soft whisper of relays, drums, gliding pens, the mechanical ticking of digital read-outs.

A woman looked up from her desk as he approached. She had silver hair, lustrous blue eyes, tinted lids, a scarlet mouth. Her figure was reed-slim her expression that of a painted doll.

One that frowned as he said, 'Are you Mary Palmer?'

'And if I am?'

'I was told you would help me, Varl.' He took a chair at her side. 'You've some answers for me.'

'I have?' Her disdain was obvious. 'And you think you can get them just by barging in here?'

'You have a nice face,' said Varl. 'Let's keep it that way. Have you a boss? An intelligent assistant? Get him.'

'My superior is — '

'Just get him.'

He arrived within minutes, tall, flustered, slowing his pace as he saw Varl. Halting he said, 'You wanted me?'

'Contact the Comptroller. Find out who I am.'

'I know who you are.'

'Then you know what I want. The girl didn't.'

'Mary is, well, a little spoiled, I guess. And she's sensitive. You upset her with your joke.'

'I wasn't joking. Your name?' Varl nodded as the man gave it. 'Well, Rastic, let's stop wasting time. We'll start with the comparisons.'

Rastic knew his job even if he couldn't keep his staff in line. Within seconds he had the images on the screen explaining as he worked.

'An image was taken from each recording and adjusted to exact dimensions. That's no proof, of course, because it washes out variances in size, but it does give a perfect silhouette-match. See?' The images flowed one into the other on the screen and became one.

'No blurring and no fringe-tint that would betray an uneven match. We can now check other details that, if the actual size was different, would not match because of ratio-design. A larger vessel would carry more guns, for example. Have more ports.'

'I understand. Get on with it.'

'Yes, well — ' Rastic shrugged. 'I can't swear to it because the courier-recording was damaged but the chances are they are one and the same vessel.'

'The odds?'

'A hundred to one they are the same. No, a thousand. Now for the spectro-scopic data. To be blunt there isn't any. Not from the alien. All we got was the normal pattern of a torpedo blast.' He anticipated the question.

'This time I'll swear to it. No contamination. The pattern was exact for the materials and quantities used in the missiles construction.'

'Anything on the flight paths?'

'This isn't my department,' said Rastic. 'Try Jac Zuber.'

He was sitting at a bench flanked with instruments, the light from the holograph he studied illuminating his face. One that belonged on a Greek statue as his body belonged in an arena.

Varl said, 'Do you like watching destruction?'

'I was checking something.' The recording froze as Zuber touched a button. 'See? That building. Now watch.'

It crumbled as the recording moved on in slow motion. Others followed it — the recording was the one gained from the courier. 'This is connected with tests for residual energy-traces. We've taken a hundred assorted samples from various sites and all point to the same thing. The lavender beams seem to induce a local explosion of savage intensity.'

'Maybe they've found a way to nullify the locking-bonds of the atomic particles so they fly apart with tremendous force. Or they could have found a method of dissolving molecular bonds and the induced heat would have an explosive effect. The results are much the same. Weaken a solid mass with a few such explosions and it will fly apart.'

As were the buildings depicted in the holograph. As it died and lights brightened the laboratory Varl said, 'What about the people?'

'Pulped. Smeared. Ripped apart.' Zuber's tone was bleak. 'Those hit didn't stand a chance.'

'And those close?' Varl added, as the other made no answer, 'I'm thinking of the residual effects. Flesh and bone might hold them better than metal and glass. Get some autopsies done with that in mind. Now what have you for me regarding the flight paths?'

Zuber had worked hard. Maybe a little too hard; driving himself when he should have rested, paying for it with small quivers of his hands, a rasp of irritation in his voice. Things Varl recognised as the man explained.

'This is sheer speculation, of course. Something in the nature of an intelligent guess. If the alien raider used hydee to run back home then it could be anywhere. But if they operated from a local base set on a galactic world then it must bear some relationship to the sites of attack,' Lines flashed on a screen as he activated a computer, the graphic display moving as he touched a control. 'Even apparently random acts are based on a certain pattern even if that pattern is unsuspected by the one concerned. What I've done is to feed in all the available data; times of the attacks as far as can be determined, their duration, planetary positions in relation to the galactic drift and so on. The computer came up with an answer.' The display halted, changed into the depiction of a world, a list of specifications. 'Plenty,' said Zuber. 'If anything this is it.'

A small, forlorn world, cold, wreathed in noxious fogs, hostile, unwanted. A bleak place barely illuminated by a distant sun.

Would the alien commander have chosen such a base?

'It's isolated,' said Zuber. 'Uninhabited. No one would see the ship arrive and leave. They could sit down and gloat at what they'd done. The fun they'd had. The filthy swine!' His anger broke through his restraint. 'When you go after them I want to go with you.'

'They needn't be there.'

'I'm talking about all the way.' Zuber looked at his hands, the fists they had formed. 'My folks were on Tusa. When Logis caught it so did they.'

A man wanting revenge and Varl knew the power of such motivation.

He said, 'I'll be on Darkside. Get there before I leave and you can come along.'

8

Darkside was the face of the moon that never saw the Earth. A torn and devastated landscape formed of craters and rifts and soaring peaks as jagged as broken glass. During the day it suffered the burning heat of the sun; at night it stared at the remote brilliance of distant stars. There was an observatory, scientific establishments, a missile testing ground and, well isolated at the base of a mountain, the training area where Varl had his volunteers.

Edallia came to meet him as they passed through the airlocks and into the sealed caverns gouged into the rock. She was drawn, a bruise on one cheek, her hair lacking its normal, golden sheen. In her office she made her report.

'Two murders. A dozen beatings. Three reported rapes.'

'Reported?'

'There have been more. All the victims

95

were from the local intake. I warned them but some are slow to learn.'

Sheep trying to match the wolves from Hell. Varl said, 'Get rid of them.'

'I've weeded out a third. The rest refuse to go and I can't make them. Wilcox has given his orders and the Comptroller is backing him. In any case we need them if we're to crew the ships getting ready.'

Varl leaned back in his chair. He was tired and felt his body twitching in a hatefully familiar rhythm. Isotopes would neutralise the synaptic misfiring, but to use them meant hospitalisation and stringent control. Things he wanted to do without.

'Get me a bottle,' he said. 'Better make it two. And a gun. A solid-shot, large calibre revolver. Better get one for yourself.'

'I'm armed.'

He saw no visible weapon but didn't doubt her word. As he didn't doubt that someone, somewhere, had paid for the bruise on her cheek.

She said, 'Do you want Ian to come along?'

'Where is he?'

'With those out on the plain.'

'Leave him.' Sabatova was of more value training the volunteers in spacesuit agility than as a bodyguard. 'Just get me what I asked for.'

The bottles held whiskey and he swallowed a quarter of one before checking the gun. It was an instrument designed to kill and shock at close-range — wild bullets were too dangerous in any ship or similar establishment. But the explosion held an advantage over a laser and the smashing impact of the bullet a greater efficiency.

'Let's go!'

The first rape victim had returned to Earth. The second, braver or more foolhardy, was working on the ships. The third was bitter.

'Two of your friends,' she said. 'I had no chance. They held me and — do you want the details?'

'Some. Where and when?'

'That's in my report.' She looked at Edallia. 'It didn't help much.'

'I'm not here to wet-nurse weaklings.

Why didn't you go for their eyes? Grab them where it hurts or — ' Edallia broke off, recognising the other's limitations. 'You know them?'

'That's in the report, too.'

'Yulin and Slade.' Edallia looked at Varl. 'They broke into her cubicle and threatened to ruin her face if she squealed. Well, she risked that. And she stayed. Given time she might learn.'

'Where are they now?'

'In the recreation room. They've just come in from outside.'

Two men who lounged on a bench, laughing, inhaling the vapours as they crushed ka'sence pods between their fingers. Others sat around forming a tight group against the rest. A division that had to be eliminated if ever the crew was to work as a unit.

Facing them Varl said, 'On your feet! Now!'

'Say's who?' Slade, the biggest of the pair, sneered as he reached for another pod. His eyes betrayed the influence of the drugged vapour — overdosed he was dangerous. 'You know what you can do, boss? You can go to hell.'

Laughter joined his own, fading as Varl stepped forward, the gun lifted in his hand. Heavy metal that slammed down to pulp the nose and mask the mouth and chin in a gush of blood.

'That's for having a big mouth.' Varl cocked the gun, the metallic sound harsh in its connotation of immediate death. 'Now get on your feet.' He turned to the woman as they obeyed. 'You're sure these are the men? No mistake?'

'None.'

'Here.' Varl handed her the gun, 'Take it. Give it to them both. In the guts.'

'Kill them?' She stared wide-eyed at the weapon, not touching it, shocked at the suggestion. 'Just shoot them? I can't, I mean — '

'I know what you mean — it's all right if someone else does it for you. You've been hurt, humiliated, but you haven't the guts for revenge.' Varl lifted the barrel of the weapon as he lowered the hammer. 'You'll return to Earth on the next ship. And you,' he stared at the two men, Yukin frozen where he stood, Slade his chin and chest masked with blood. 'You go back to Hell.'

From those standing around someone said, 'You promised us amnesty.'

'For what you'd done. Play games now and you pay for it.' Varl moved, slowly, the gun menacing them all. 'This is the last chance you get. I'll kill the next one who steps out of line. Now move! Mix! All of you! Get suited up and get outside! As soon as a ship's ready we get into action!'

Back in the office Varl took another drink. His hands shook a little and he stared at them, controlling them with his will until they steadied. He felt cheated, drained, angry with the woman for having shown herself to be weak. There should have been the roar of the gun, the smashing impact of lead, blood, pain and sudden death. Hard, rough justice; a lesson far more effective than vocal threats.

'She couldn't do it.' Edallia had guessed what he was thinking. 'You can't condition people to obey the dictates of law and order all their lives then expect them to change at a word. What about the other one?'

'Send her back too.'

'Without a chance for revenge?'

'Has she asked for it? Tried to get it? No? Then send her back.'

'She's a technician and good at her job.'

'Then let her work at it but she doesn't travel with us.' Varl reached for the bottle then changed his mind. 'Get me Orme at the shipyard.'

He was absent from his office and, while waiting for contact to be made, Edallia said, 'They won't understand it down there. About the women, I mean. Why penalise them for obeying the rules?'

'They and others were raped. If they liked it then why complain? If they didn't and kept quiet about it they may have learned not to let it happen again or be waiting to settle it later. That is understandable. But those three made an issue of it. By reporting it they appealed for help. They showed they couldn't stand on their own feet. I don't need them.' Varl looked at his hands again then jerked to his feet to pace the office. 'What the hell's keeping Orme?'

He came on a few minutes later, an elderly man with grizzled hair and eyes meshed with lines. Without preamble he said, 'Don't keep pushing me. We're working as fast as we can.'

'On what?'

'The hydee adaptations you ordered. They — '

'Can wait,' snapped Varl. 'Something's come up. What I need now are ships ready to move. Ones with plenty of firepower and with special instrumentation. Infra-red detectors, variable mass-gauges, sonar equipment — everything necessary to find something that may be hidden. Can do?'

'Sure, in time. The instrumentation is easy and we can use the ships we've already adapted for extra fire-power.'

'How much time?' Varl shook his head at the answer and leaned closer to the screen. 'This takes priority. I need one ship by tomorrow, two if you can manage it. One can be used as a backup so can be skimped. The other needs to have the hydee interrupter we talked about.'

'I told you, the cascade — '

'Forget that. Just the interrupter. You've got twenty hours.'

Varl killed the screen before the other could argue and sat, fighting his tension, the hateful twitching born of fatigue and frustration. The product of his own impatience, but he hadn't believed the doctors when they had tried to assure him that, given time, all would be well. The time they had spoken of was his life and the peace they promised lay beyond the grave. He had chosen a different route; battling the monster which rode him, the legacy of the alien blast.

One he saw again as he closed his eyes, opening them as he felt something thrust into his hands.

A bottle and Edallia had given it to him. She said, 'Calm down, Kurt. Get drunk if you have to but stop burning yourself out.' Then, hesitantly, she suggested, 'How about me calling a medic? A shot might help you get some rest.'

'Forget it.' The whiskey burned his mouth and slid down into his stomach. It could have been water. 'Contact Polar North. Talk to Jac Zuber. Ask if he's determined anything as to the time-factor of the raids. If he hasn't get him working on it.'

'Time-factor?'

'He'll understand. And tell him he's got fifteen hours.'

Varl stepped to the door as she busied herself with the communicator. His restlessness demanded action and he found it by moving around the installation checking on the progress of those in training. The schedule was hard; a barely broken grind of suit-drill, gun-drill, emergency procedures and simulated battle-conditions. In the cramped confines of a facsimile vessel the volunteers ran, dodged, responded to a variety of incidents.

An explosion, the blare of alarms, a voice rising over the din.

'Hit in section-nine. Compartments eight to twelve open to vacuum. Attack continuing.'

Doors slammed shut trapping those within the ruined chambers. Gunners aimed at the simulated target and maintained fire while their comrades died from wounds, loss of air, horrible burns. Others ran to locks to confine and repair the damage.

Another alarm, the facsimile jerking as if hit by a savage explosion, more orders, more frenzied activity. Apparent chaos but Varl could recognise the ordered rhythm of organised response.

To the officer in charge he said, 'How are they making out?'

'Pretty good, so far. As far as basic training goes, that is, but — '

His shrug was expressive and Varl knew what he meant. As yet this was a game; one the volunteers were learning to play. There should be real blood, real pain and danger of injury and death. Some would fall but the rest would learn. Failing actual combat he should have put the rapists among them and had them blown apart by a bomb to simulate a real event. He had missed the chance and wondered how many other mistakes he was making.

In a place covered by a thick mat another instructor was teaching unarmed combat which, so far as those from Hell were concemed, was like teaching a chicken to lay eggs.

'Most when they fight use only two weapons,' he was saying. 'They think only of their hands and then in terms of fists. Others, like savate fighters, put the greater importance on their feet. But an arm has an elbow as well as a hand and a leg has a knee as well as a foot. And there is always the head that can be a devastating weapon when skillfully applied. A trained fighter in unarmed combat knows how to use them all.'

But a real fighter, a killer, would always use a weapon of some kind if given the chance. Even a handful of dirt thrown into an opponent's eyes would yield the needed advantage.

Varl moved on. He felt hot and dirty and some of the hateful twitching still remained. In the office Edallia watched as he took another drink.

'It's time we went to bed,' she said. 'I can relax you more than what's in that bottle.' She came towards him, hands reaching, her own need plain in her eyes. 'And you can relax me. Kurt?'

'You smell,' he said. 'We both smell.

First let's get a bath.'

He stripped in his cubicle and padded to the communal showers with a towel draped over his arm. Showered, clean, he dried himself and headed back to his room. As he neared it a man stepped through the door. Slade, his nose swollen, clown-like with its dressing of white tape. But there was nothing of the clown in his smile.

'Got you, you bastard!'

Yulin had followed Slade and stood a yard behind him and to one side. Weapons were not allowed the volunteers but both men were armed; Slade with a jagged scrap of metal, Yulin with the leg of a chair that he hefted like a club.

'Get him, Slade. Don't waste time talking.'

Good advice and Varl took it. As Slade came forward in a lunging run he fired the pistol he held beneath the cover of the towel. The bullet slammed into Slade's chest, halting his rush, sending him to lie jerking in his death throes on the floor.

'No!' Yulin halted his own forward movement, lifting both hands, head thrown back and mouth open as he begged for his life. 'No! Please! I'll — '

The bullet drilled between his parted lips to geyser from the top of his skull in an eruption of blood, brain and splinters of bone.

'Kurt!' Edallia came running. Like himself she was naked but for a towel. Her eyes widened as she saw the bodies. 'Are you hurt?'

'No. Where did you put the whiskey?'

'In my room, but — '

'Let's get to it.'

He led her from the scene feeling calm now, relaxed. The dead could lie as a lesson to others. Later they could be thrown out with the rest of the garbage.

9

Orme delivered the ships an hour before the deadline; the *Keil* incomplete, the *Dalio* incorporating all Varl had ordered. Inspecting it was like stepping into a dream; one with solid walls and compartments, turrets and passages, all empty of life now but thronged with ghosts and memories.

'You'll notice improvements,' said Orme. 'The *Odile* was good but this is better.'

Incorporating data won from his raving delirium when he had refought the aliens in mental turmoil. Kalif had been clever and must have ordered their construction without delay. Utilising the information to make the new vessels the most potent instruments of destruction in space.

But ships were only as good as their crews and Edallia listened to Varl's orders with mounting anger.

'Not going? You're leaving me behind?'

'You and all the other women.'

'Why? Aren't we good enough? We can fight as well as anyone and what about ship-tension? How are you going to handle that?'

'With work.' He was blunt. 'There'll be no time for dalliance. The crews have to be whipped into shape before we reach Reitty. I've ordered the instructors to pick the best on a sixty-twenty ratio.'

The twenty from Hell the rest local volunteers. The wolves would stiffen the sheep and yet be in the minority.

Varl explained, 'We haven't had time to establish the kind of discipline I need. This expedition will supply it. Orme will supply a couple of ships for training.' Real ships and real weapons; as different to the facsimilies as a femmikin in a pleasure-parlour was different to a real flesh and blood woman. 'I'm putting you in charge of that. When I return I want everything ready to move.'

'And if you don't?'

'Come back?' Varl shrugged. 'If I'm dead I won't give a damn what happens. Now let's get to it — we haven't much time.'

Zuber had dictated that. Established in the *Dalio* with his papers and charts and computer-data he looked at Varl as he slumped into a chair.

'You look all in.'

'Never mind that. Have you checked the figures?'

'A dozen times using different variables each run. The attack-pattern seems random but, as I explained, few things really are. More data would yield greater probability but I think — '

'Get on with it.'

'Yes.' Zuber looked at his findings. If he was annoyed at the interruption he didn't show it. Already he had learned that Varl was a man of little patience. 'If we hit at the time decided on there is a good chance the alien ship will be at its base. Three days later it could be out on another raid.' He added, 'Assuming Reitty is their base.'

And assuming there was only one ship. If one was on a raid and the other on the planet the punitive force stood a good chance of being caught between a rock and a hard place. Things Varl considered

111

as he took his place at the controls. As the pre-flight checks were being made he contacted the other ship.

'Captain Chatto? We are about to embark. Repeat your orders.'

'We leave five minutes after you do and emerge well away from the target. If possible we establish visual contact and maintain radio silence.'

'And if you spot an alien?'

'We run for it, but — '

'You don't like it,' said Varl. 'I know, but I've no time for heroes. You are my back-up. You do as I say at all times. You watch. You learn. You come to the rescue only when I ask for it.'

'And if you're destroyed?'

'That'll be too bad — for me. Stand by now. We leave in fifteen. Mark!'

Seconds in which to scan the control panel and check that all was in the green. As a tell-tale flared into ruby life a thin, keening whine filled the ship. A note that grew shrill, stinging the ears before it climbed above audible range.

In the engine room a paradox came into being.

Kreutzal's invention was a machine that had no moving parts. A complex mesh of energy-fields were created within the framework of symmetrical coils immersed in liquid hydrogen and ringed with massive armatures. A super-cooled conductor will circulate current without loss. Shape those conductors to harmonise with others of similar nature to form a region of mutual induction and a situation is created which, if enough power is supplied, leads to an irresistible force meeting an immovable object.

Power, seeking to escape its artificial confines, formed the very situation which made it impossible for it to do so. Intense field-pressures built to form a node of complexity that could not exist within the framework of the normal universe. It could not dissipate. It could not change. It could only go somewhere else.

Into hyperspace and with it the engine that created it, the ship in which it was held, everything contained within the hull. A portion of normal space thrown into limbo — a region that was still a mystery but which, Varl knew, held its own, peculiar horror.

'Watch your levels!' He snarled as a red warning light flashed on the panel. 'Roderigo!'

'Sorry, sir.' The engineer's voice held strain. 'Flux zeroed.'

'Keep it that way. Check those verniers. Life-support! Check your systems!' Varl was taking no more chances than he had to on an untried vessel. 'Segman! Stand by for time and distance correlation.'

'Mark, sir?'

'Five!!'

Varl counted then the screens showed the vista of normal space. Behind them the moon looked like a rugged ball, the Earth a glowing orb lying to one side. As the navigator checked the apparent size of both and made his calculation as to the distance the ship had travelled while the hydee had been engaged Varl watched his every move. A good man, one trained in Polar North. He would make another half-dozen checks then should be able to put the ship just where it was wanted to go.

As Burchard could put his torpedoes.

The mercenary smiled as Varl entered the firing-room and lifted a hand in greeting. The uniform he wore made him similar to the rest but his eyes set him apart. His eyes and humourless smile and the record of killing that had ended with him running to Hell.

'All fine here, sir.'

'How are you manning the guns?'

'Our kind on the laser cannon — they've learned to be quick on the trigger. Others handling the loading and fusing of the torps.'

'Change them around and keep them mixed. I want all to be as good as each other.'

Burchard shrugged. 'Putting horns on a sheep doesn't make it a ram. Blood, now, that's different. Once they learn it's kill or be killed — well, I guess you know that.'

'I know it.' Varl looked at the instruments filling the room, the computer-guidance mechanisms, the rangefinder and automatic relays. 'What happens if this lot gets knocked out?'

'Individual systems. While a gun can work it can be fired. This just coordinates the whole.' His gesture embraced the room. His hand lowered as he added, 'Why the questions? You think it could happen?'

'Run drills assuming it has. And I want individual hand-projector training. Make them wear suits, put them in the dark with faulted weapons, make sure they know how to fix them and fast. You don't have to be gentle.'

'You're after something.' The mercenary smiled as he thought about it. 'That's the kind of training we used to give recruits when planning a raid. Is that what you've got in mind? A raid?'

'Maybe.'

'Then our kind can do without it. They don't need it.'

'They can get lazy and they can forget. Like you.'

'Meaning?'

'On my ship there is no 'their kind' and 'our kind'. We are one working together and you'd better remember it. As you'd better remember something else. I'm the captain of the *Dalio* and the commander of the whole expedition. I'd hate for you to forget that.'

Burchard thought of Slade and Yukin, the way they had died. He said, 'No, Captain, I'm not likely to forget that.'

'Good.' Varl looked around the room. 'We're wasting time. Get on with those drills.'

Hydee travel was fast but Reitty was distant and there was time to rove the ship and make endless checks of what it contained. More time to sit at the controls and stare at the formless grey swirl of hyperspace filling the screens. A swirl that needn't be formless at all but a riot of colour and vistas which the human visual range simply could not comprehend. Or perhaps the brain converted the images relayed to it into a harmless nothingness in order to maintain sanity.

Limbo — where the dead could wander through all eternity. Where thoughts could take form and become ghastly things of nightmare or constructions of unbelievable beauty. Realms of loveliness inhabited by creatures of shimmering effulgence or reeking chasms in which lurked terrifying monsters.

Things best not dwelt on. In the engine

room Roderigo tended the humming unit of the hydee and checked the operation of an enigmatic unit to one end of the chamber. One that seemed to dampen all activity so that loneliness became as much a part of the vessel as the cold metal of decks and bulkheads.

'I know what it does and what it's for but I'll never get to like it,' he admitted. 'The damned thing's like a sponge.'

'That's because it's operating on reversed polarity.' Varl crossed to it, laid a hand on it. 'Turn it the other way and you'd think you stood in a crowd. We used it as bait. This way it protects us.'

From the thing that lurked in limbo. One that existed in four dimensions and turned living humans into things of screaming horror. Another danger to add to the rest but one they had learned to live with helped by the psychic emission amplifying projector; the peap. The alien raiders were something else.

'They could be trapped,' said Zuber, 'If more than one followed you through they may not be able to get back.'

'Then why the delay before the attacks?'

118

'Maybe they needed repairs. Or they could have tried to get back and couldn't make it. If so they could have settled for making the best of things in this universe. It's a possibility.'

'You believe it?'

'No,' admitted Zuber. 'I've been doing some studies with reference to their potential social structure. An intelligent creature acts intelligently because it's intelligent,' he explained. 'At least that's the way the socio-technicians like to put it. Act like a cruel, heartless bastard and the chance is that you are one. Destroy like an insane barbarian and — ' He shrugged. 'You can fill in the rest.'

'They can't be barbarians,' said Varl. 'It takes a high technology to build spaceships.'

'It takes a high technology to make guns, needles, knives, axes, but savages used them. They bought them from traders.' Zuber pushed aside his papers. 'We need more data. How can we guess what aliens will do when we can't even understand our own life-forms? Termites share the same world, the same environment, are made of the same basic materials and have been around longer than we have — yet we can't reach them. What do they think when we level one of their mounds to make way for a road? And bees — how do they feel when we steal their honey?'

'You're saying?'

'Nothing, I guess. Nothing new, that is.' Zuber took a deep breath and rubbed at his eyes. 'I'm just trying to figure out what we're up against.'

'I can tell you that.' Varl was blunt. 'We're up against the things which stamped the life out of your folks as if they'd been dirt. Just hang on to that. Keep it in mind. Your folks and all the others that have died because of the aliens. With luck we'll meet them. When we do it's them or us. I want it to be us.'

'Soon?'

'In two days we'll be at Reitty.'

Time for final checks and drills then nothing but the long, dragging period of waiting. Time for Varl to explain the entire purpose of the expedition.

'We want to capture the raider if we find him.' The intercom carried his voice all over the vessel. 'Undamaged if we can

120

but a wreck if it can't be avoided. We need to learn from it. The *Dalio* will make the attempt and the *Keil* will hold back to give us help and rescue if we need it. I tell you this so you'll know we aren't alone. I want no wild firing. No hysterical outbursts. We take prisoners if we can and you will follow orders at all times.' He added, 'You are a military unit and will act like one. All of you. That's all.'

From his chair Segman said, 'Ten minutes to emergence, Captain.'

'Check all scanners, Koslenko.'

'In the green and triggered.'

'Canale?'

'Ready, sir.'

To take over if anything should happen to Varl. To receive reports and transmit orders and keep the ship running as an operational unit. As the others could do — if they had to — no man was or should be indispensable.

'Five minutes.' Segman ran his tongue over lips grown suddenly dry.

Varl said, 'No need to count, mister. We can all see the chronometer.'

The swinging hand that counted off the

seconds and was, in a way, the metronome of life itself. Now they were safe, snug, warm. Soon they could be torn apart, drifting in space, dead or dying.

'Battle alert.' Varl broke the silence. 'Seal suits and switch to combat-web communication. Thirty seconds!'

An eternity and then, suddenly, the screen cleared and Reitty lay before them.

The world and something else.

10

It was a flash, gone as soon as seen, an impression of shimmering gold without real shape or form. Something limned against the mist wreathing the planet as if it had just arrived or left.

'Koslenko?'

'An object. Mass about equal to our own. High density. Moving fast.'

'Direction?' Varl bared his teeth as the officer shrugged. 'What the hell's the matter with you? Which way did it go?'

'Away.' Koslenko gestured at his panel. 'As if it shrank.'

An illusion; massive acceleration would have produced a similar effect or the sudden enveloping of mist and cloud.

Either way they had no choice; if the alien had left on another raid they had time to find its base and prepare a trap against its return. If it had just arrived they had to hit fast before its scanners could warn of impending danger.

'Check the planetary surface. Canale! Take over! Put us into a scanning orbit.'

Varl leaned back as the other obeyed, eyes on the screens, the vista they portrayed. Mist like an endless sea that covered rook and ice and jagged mountains. Lakes of fuming vapours and chasms that held the ravaged face of tormented nature.

Before him signal-lamps flashed and winked. He ignored them. Canale was in control and to override him was to diminish his confidence and demean his standing. Only by doing could a man learn.

'Something.' Koslenko lifted a hand. 'Steady now. Circle,' he grunted as Canale obeyed. 'Look!'

A monitor screen flickered then steadied to show a rift edged with rugged peaks. The colours were strange, changing as the compensators adapted them to human vision; blues and whites and murky greys and, among them, touches of red.

'High-temperature points,' said Koslenko. 'The infra-red's picking them up.'

'Natural eruptions?'

'I doubt it.' Koslenko adjusted a control as he answered Varl's question. 'They're too local for that. Too large to be human. The heat's more in the conductive range and fading. As if a big fire has recently been extinguished,' he explained. 'We could be looking at the cooling ash.'

Or the residuals left by a departing vessel. One which even now could be on a mission to kill and burn and destroy another helpless community.

'We've got them,' whispered Segman. 'By God, we've got them!'

Or were being invited into a trap. They had spotted the alien — had they been spotted in turn? If so the raider could be waiting until they landed then to come in with ravening beams of destruction. Varl glanced at the chronometer. The *Keil* should have emerged by now and be waiting far distant if Chatto had followed his orders. To break radio silence was to run a risk but he decided to take it.

'*Dalio* to *Keil*,' he snapped. 'Don't answer just listen. We're going in but we could have been spotted. Move in and

125

orbit Reitty. Don't get too close. Don't stay too long. Give us ten minutes then back off. Out.'

A cover and a diversion? If the raider had spotted them they would have retreated to later return ready for attack. Seeing the twin vessel they would think it the same. Once it departed they would feel safe. Landing they would be caught unawares.

Varl said, 'Battle stations! We're going down!'

Taking over the controls he headed the ship towards the planet. Mist came closer, enveloped them, blinding the scanners until electronic magic adjusted the images. Slow — the stream of millipulses governing the hydee allowed of slow and close manoeuvring and rocket power permitted a tighter control in case of need.

From his position Koslenko said, '*Keil* in position, sir.'

'Below?'

'Nothing new. It's all — no! Captain!'

Varl had seen it; a sudden flare of released fury, which burned in eye-bright splendour. An energy-discharge reaching towards them, that would have hit them but for the speed of his reaction. One born of training and tension and the need to survive. Even as Koslenko spoke he had hit the button controlling the newly installed interrupter unit on the hydee.

'All units! Fire!'

To those within the ship nothing seemed to have happened. To an outsider the *Dalio* seemed to flicker and that was all. But during that flicker the power of the hydee had thrown the vessel far from its previous position — and then returned it to where it had been. Time for the energy-blast to pass through empty air. For any missiles to have done the same.

Time for the ship's own weapons to rain a hail of destructive fury on the ground below.

Fire bloomed, died, leaving gaping craters and open fissures. Ripping apart the face of masking cliffs and turning the hidden defences into clouds of scintillating vapour. Pulverising. Wiping out of existence anything the aliens might have left behind.

'Cease firing!' Varl glowered at the

screens. The destruction had been necessary but, aside from saving the ship, had accomplished nothing. To Canale he said, 'Land. Find a cavern of some kind and put the ship into it. I want us out of sight and under cover. Burchard! Assemble the landing party!'

He led the way from the port, suited, the weight of the rocket-projector heavy in his hands. Beside him Zuber grunted as he stumbled and almost fell.

'Damn! I — '

'No talking!' Varl was sharp as the voice came over his radio. 'I want the channel kept clear. Just watch where you tread.'

On ice and crumbling rock. Over ridges and between narrow fissures. The *Dalio* had been grounded well away from the area, tucked beneath an overhanging mass of rock, the mechanisms silent, the vessel dead. Canale was at the controls, Koslenko at his scanners, Burchard manning his guns. The rest of the crew followed Varl to set the trap he had designed.

A ring of men, armed, watching, waiting for the alien to return. Hiding in cracks, blending into the terrain. Too small to be easily spotted and yet with enough combined firepower to do what needed to be done. Once settled all they had to do was wait.

Wait and hope the alien would return to its base. That it would be careless or overconfident. That it would be alone and, above all, that it wouldn't be too long.

Locked in the confines of a suit, imagination became prey to bizarre imagination and outré fears. An itch became a mind-destroying torment. The sense of loneliness turned into a nightmare of having been abandoned, forgotten, left to rot on a hostile world. Muscles began to twitch and deep-buried anxieties surfaced to gnaw with relentless teeth at the surface of the mind.

'Easy.' Varl had judged the mounting tension and broke radio-silence to ease the strain. A calculated risk but not to take it was to invite hysteria or numbed incomprehension when the time to act arrived. 'Check your weapons and relax your muscles.' He added, with rough humour, 'Just think of this as the hard part.'

Waiting while the sun lowered and the air grew bleak. Until the dawn came to pale the mist and reveal near-forgotten detail.

Then, an hour later, the alien was above them.

There was beauty in it and menace; the shimmering iridescence of a serpent's scales coupled with the venom of its fangs. Varl watched as it slowly lowered in a haze of gold. A shimmer that turned suddenly green.

'They know!' Varl swung his projector into line. 'One through fifteen fire and duck!'

The numbers denoted pairs and thirty rockets streamed from the projectors to blossom against the bizarre hull in flowers of ravening fury. As they faded the green shimmer vanished to be replaced by searing lavender beams.

'Now!'

Varl squeezed the release and sent rockets lancing towards the alien hull. Unprotected now, they had lowered their defences, and he saw blue-white flame sear at the golden surface. Burn and spread and expand in plumes of incandescent vapour.

'More! All of you — keep firing!'

The one chance they would have to hurt and cripple, wreck and destroy. To bring the alien down and render it helpless. To kill. To revenge!

Over the radio he heard animal-like sounds as men vented their rage. Of Zuber mouthing the names of his dead as he flung destruction at the alien. Of other sounds, fainter; the screams and cries of those wounded by the lavender beams. The sacrifices used to gain a vulnerable target.

Then, as the beams lashed out again, Varl yelled into his radio.

'Canale! Get up and over here! Fast!'

The alien was rising, firing as it rose, ice and dirt pluming on all sides, blood mixed with the pulverised rock, bone ground into minute fragments of ruby-tinged white.

Rising too fast and too high for the projectors to be effective — the very trails of the missiles betraying their position.

'Cease firing!' Varl tasted blood as

something smashed close to him and sent him rolling. 'Canale! Where the hell are you?'

A ship tucked under rock and ice. Barely crewed. Dead and needing to be woken into life. An easy target as it rose — but other help was at hand.

The *Keil* — hurtling from space like a thrown spear directly at the alien.

Fire preceded it; the ravening blast of torpedoes, the searing beams of laser-cannon. Steam spouted from the distant side of a peak as gunners missed but enough fury struck home to send the alien vessel veering as, too late, its defensive screen flared green.

Green then vivid white as it crashed against the side of the canyon to fall, spinning to the ground below. To expand in a blinding gout of flame which filled the air with a rain of hurtling fragments.

'The fool!' Varl jerked to his feet trembling in his anger. 'The damned fool!'

'He saved us.' Zuber was at his side. 'If Chatto hadn't come in when he did — '

'We wanted that ship. We had it. A couple of well-aimed torps would have finished the job. Now we've got nothing.' Varl glared at the scatter of debris, the shape of the *Keil* now coming in to land, the *Dalio* now in view. Into his radio he snapped, 'All hands suited and out! I want to see what can be found.'

Dead men lying where they had fallen or been thrown like broken dolls far to one side. Some seemed to be asleep in their suits, others had been torn apart to die screaming in a welter of broken flesh and bone.

Two thirds of the attack-force had died; the flames from their pyre illuminated the scene as the rest continued the search.

Finding dirt, debris, twisted and torn scraps of metal. Blobs like rubbish that had once been carefully fabricated artifacts. Things seared and burned beyond any recognition mixed with garbage coated with ash and char to litter the area.

And, at its edge, resting against the foot of a peak, the ripped and broken fragment of a once-golden hull and, within it, something that moaned and gibbered and was, incredibly, alive.

11

'A man?' Edallia was incredulous. 'You found a man in that ship?'

Varl nodded.

'You mean a real, human male?'

'One as human as I am.' Varl halted and turned to lean on the parapet of the wall edging the balcony on which they stood. Distance made the figures in the streets below look like scurrying ants. 'He was badly hurt and it was a miracle he survived the crash. I cut him free, put him in an emergency-sac, and rushed him here.'

To Franzel the nearest world to Reitty with good hospital facilities. With good, clean air also and a sun which tinted the air with a warm haze of tangerine. It was low now, almost touching the horizon, and the shadow of the building stretched out like a truncated cone over the city.

Edallia said, 'Kalif didn't like it. He figured you should have sent the prisoner to Earth.'

'He wouldn't have made it.'

'Not in an emergency-sac?' The lift of her eyebrows told him she knew better. 'Well, if he's fit now he can travel. There's a lot they want to ask him.'

'They can keep wanting.'

'You'd defy the Comptroller?'

Varl shrugged; three times now he had ignored orders to send the prisoner to Polar North. 'Any news on the other stuff?'

'Little of value. The alloy of the hull is similar to our own but with a higher percentage of titanium and gold. Maybe they used the gold as an outer plating to provide a good conductor for their defensive screen. It seems to be that way. The technicians are still working on the rest.' She hesitated then added, 'Some of the blobs could have been bodies.'

'Human?'

'There's no way of telling but the technicians are checking the DNA. I left before they had an answer.' Arriving in the *Egon*, a matching vessel to the *Dalio* and *Keil*, its hull packed with crew and supplies. She added, 'Orme has two more on the stocks but I didn't think you'd want me to wait. Anyway our friends from Hell were getting restless for action.'

'They'll get it soon. What do you think of Marne?'

'He handled the *Egon* well enough. A regular but he seems to know his job. I guess he's as good a captain as any other. He'd like me to be a part of his crew.'

'You want that?'

'I'm riding with you.' Her tone brooked of no argument. 'I've worked out the crew-dispositions for your inspection and agreement and supplies are being transferred. I want to be alone with you, but before that, I'd like to see the prisoner.'

He sat in a small room fitted with bare necessities; a bed, a chair, toilet facilities, a washbowl set beneath a faucet. There were no windows. In the shadowless glow thrown by an overhead plate he seemed beaten, forlorn, oblivious of the eyes studying him through the one-way glass.

'A Caucasian male.' Doctor Wayne supplied the details. 'About thirty years of age, dark hair, brown eyes, skin slightly pigmented. Probably of Asian antecedents. His hands show signs of having done hard manual work in the past but are now soft. The palms are broad,' he explained, 'the fingers slightly spatulate. The body bears the scars of severe whipping, again mostly done in the past. The general physical condition is good — aside from the effects of his recent injuries. The main trouble seems to lie in his mind.'

'Shock,' commented Edallia. 'To be expected. Can he talk?'

'Perfectly. His name is Amra Kendrick.'

'He told you that? You could understand him?'

'As well as he can understand me. There is no difficulty in communication. What is puzzling is his reaction to certain members of the hospital staff. Nurses,' he added. 'He seems to be afraid of them.'

Varl said, 'Anything else?'

'Nothing aside from an unusually high testosterone content.' Wayne glanced at the slumped figure beyond the glass. 'As far as I can tell he isn't dangerous, but if you want guards they can be supplied.'

'That won't be necessary. Thank you, Doctor.' As the man walked away Varl said, 'I told him no more than he had to know, that's why he wasn't surprised Kendrick could understand him.'

'But how? An alien — it doesn't make sense. But if he's human he can't be an alien — yet you found him in the raider's ship.' Edallia shook her head, annoyed at herself for her lack of comprehension. 'Let's go and talk to him.'

He rose as they entered, Varl in the lead, smiling as he straightened.

'Kurt, my friend, it is good to see you again. The waiting is long but — ' He broke off as Edallia came into his full view. 'My lady!' He bowed from the waist, both arms extended at his sides, head lowered, knees bent in the classical posture of obeisance. He backed as she approached, a man terrified, cringing as if he expected a blow. 'Forgive your humble chiro. I should have died with my mistress but I lived. For this I merit punishment.'

'What the hell are you talking about?' Edallia was curt. She moved forward, tall, regal in her gown of emerald edged with gold. A costume designed to accentuate her femininity and worn for Varl's benefit. 'Are you crazy?'

'My lady! Forgive me!'

'For what?' Impatience sharpened her tone. 'Look at me. Lift your head, damn you. That's better.' She stared into the man's face recognising the abject terror in his eyes. 'What are you afraid of? Me? Why?'

'My lady, you — ' Kendrick broke off, the words clogging in his throat. 'I am not to blame,' he almost screamed. 'The fault was not mine. I beg you, my lady, please be merciful!'

'Mad.' Edallia stepped back shaking her head. 'He's mad. Now I know what the doctor was getting at. Does he act this way with the nurses?'

'He isn't so intense.' Varl jerked his head towards the door in a signal for her to leave. Outside the room he said, 'They wear greens — the usual uniform. You're dressed like a highborn lady. That gown must remind him of something.' He looked through the one-way glass to where Kendrick had again slumped on his chair. 'It proves a suspicion I have.'

'You know more than you're telling,' she accused. 'You've talked with him before. He knew you. Called you his friend. What the hell's going on?'

'Nothing you need worry about.'

'I want to know. I've a right to know.'

'Later.' Varl looked down the passage to where a nurse had halted looking at them. 'Ask Doctor Wayne to attend me,' he said. 'Tell him programme twelve — he'll understand.' To Edallia he said, 'Get back to the ships. Speed up the transfer and get everything ready for us to leave. When you've done that come to my room in the Jurgan Hotel. Number 327.'

★　★　★

It was dark when she arrived, the room illuminated only by starlight streaming through the high windows to fabricate an elaborate chiaroscuro on the walls. A tracery of black and silver that held the delicacy of lace. Almost buried in a deep chair Varl seemed a part of it, a man-like fabrication with a face patterned with cobwebs.

'Kurt?' Edallia moved cautiously towards him, cursing as her foot hit something

140

that chimed and rolled. A glass — the air held the taint of whiskey.

'Kurt! Put on a light!'

It bloomed from hidden sources as he obeyed; a pale, warm pink which gave the impression of a summer's dawn. Soft but enough to banish the cobwebs, the traceries of lace.

'Nice.' She assessed the room with a sweep of her eyes. 'A suite, eh? Well, why not — Earth Confederation's footing the bill. How about some champagne?'

'Order it if you want.' Varl gestured towards the communicator. 'Or will you settle for what I've got?'

'You've been drinking.' She picked up the glass she had almost broken and poured herself whiskey from the bottle. 'Why?'

'I've just tortured a man to the point of death — you want a better reason?'

'Kendrick?' She drank and shrugged. 'You didn't torture him. Wayne did that if anyone. Programme twelve,' she mused. 'I've heard about that. The use of drugs to induce shock-therapy and break down mental inhibitions. Sometimes it's used to break down a suspect's resistance and make him talk. Well, did you learn anything new?'

'Just verification of what I suspected. That wasn't why I ordered programme twelve. If Kendrick is to be of any use to us he had to get rid of previous indoctrination. I don't want him terrified of women.'

She said, dryly, 'You don't need programme twelve for that. There are easier ways.' Lifting her glass she added, 'Here's to them.'

'You don't understand.' Varl dropped a hand to his side and lifted it towards her. He held a thin, silver, metal band. It was almost an inch wide, engraved and, closed, would have fitted snugly around a neck. 'Kendrick was wearing this when I found him. I cut it free. Guess what it is.'

'An ornament?' She examined it, frowning at the engraving, narrowing her eyes to read the script. 'No. It's a collar of some kind.' She met Varl's eyes. 'A slave collar?'

He nodded.

'Are you saying that Kendrick was a slave?'

'A chiro,' he said. 'They're known as chiros. Apt, really, chiro means hand. That's what they are — hands. Hand, slave, chiro, it's all the same to them. Now do you understand?'

The collar. The cringing deference. The terror he had shown. The talk of guilt and merited punishment. His fear of women. Other things.

Edallia looked again at the collar then dropped it on the table. 'A slave,' she said. 'One belonging to a woman. Someone in that alien ship — but it doesn't make sense. Why would ordinary women attack burn and destroy?'

'Did I say they were ordinary?' Varl poured himself a drink and sipped it as he stared at the windows, the stars beyond. 'Zuber was right in his guess,' he said. 'Two ships followed me through the rift. One I destroyed the other holed up on Reitty. There was damage that had to be repaired and something else. Kendrick couldn't tell me exactly what — as a slave he was just a piece of convenient furniture. He was there just to clean and entertain. He wasn't alone.'

'Ship-boys? But — '

'Call them pets,' Varl suggested. 'Good at massage and other things. If you wanted such how would you operate?'

'Pick them for a high sexual proclivity. Help them along with cantharides, boost them with testosterone — ' She broke off, remembering what Wayne had said. 'What happens when they're worn out?'

'Dumped — they're only slaves, remember. Sold for dog-meat or put to work in the fields. That's why Kendrick was so terrified when he saw you. He expected the worst.'

'And now?'

'We may have calmed him. Broken his indoctrination.' Varl sipped at his whiskey. 'We'll know for sure tomorrow when he's had time to settle.'

Tomorrow, but that was another day. Edallia moved restlessly about the room, touching a small vase, a delicate statuette, a block of crystal in which blooms had been encapsulated in unfading beauty. She felt excited, stimulated by novel images. A ship crewed by women with men as their doting slaves. Amazon-crews weren't unknown but among them men had no place. On some worlds matriarchal societies had long been established, as had the practice of polyandry, but it wasn't the same. A woman could head a household or have multiple husbands, but slaves? Men to grovel, plead, beg, obey?

Watching her Varl said, 'It gets you, doesn't it?'

'What?'

'The prospect of power. Of total domination. That's why thrones are so popular — everyone wants to be the one to give the orders.'

'That's different. I was thinking of — never mind.' Edallia kicked at a cushion and sent it rolling over the carpet to land against a wall. To change the subject she said, 'Where's Zuber? I haven't seen him since I arrived and I've some stuff for him.'

'Put it in the *Dalio*.' Varl added, 'I sent him to Polar North shortly after we found Kendrick. We'll leave when he gets back. In the meantime — ' His gesture embraced the suite. 'Let's enjoy what we have.'

The softness, the comfort, the superb view. The drinks and the meal Varl ordered and which was served by deferential waiters moving as softly as ghosts. Then, later, music and the interplay of colours as a visual symphony painted the walls with gleaming luminescence.

'Nice.' Edallia stretched like a cat. 'Why can't we all live like this all of the time?'

'You'd like to?'

'No.' She was honest. 'I'd get bored.'

She was still restless and Varl could guess why. He said, as she rose to pace the floor, 'You don't need a whip to win a man.'

'Why did you say that?'

'And you don't have to drug one to make him able to perform.'

'Not now,' she admitted. 'But later?'

'To hell with later.' His arms closed around her. 'Let's live for now.'

12

Zuber arrived three days later with bales of equipment and a personal order from Nasir Kalif.

'He wants the prisoner, Kurt. The technicians are itching to get their hands on him and the Council is riding him hard. He would have sent a squad of armed men but he figured it would do no good.'

'He was right. I need Kendrick. Did you get the information?'

'Some, the rest is tucked away in there.' Zuber waved a hand at the bales. 'I had no time for a close check as I had the relevant recordings copied. I can run them while we're on our way.'

'Run what?' Edallia entered the compartment. She looked tired, drawn, her femininity masked by the uniform she wore. Pants and tunic belted at the waist — the common garb of men and women alike. 'I've been to see Amra. He wasn't too easy but at least he didn't cringe. I guess programme twelve did its job.'

'Kendrick?' Zuber looked from one to the other. 'You've managed to break through? Good. Now, maybe, we can get some real answers.'

Varl left him busy with his equipment, leading the way from the ship with Edallia at his side. Outside Chatto and Marne stood in the open a small group of crewmen standing to one side. Two of them were bound, the rest were armed. Thieves caught pilfering the *Egon's* stores now waiting judgment.

'Let them go,' said Chatto. 'Send them back to Hell.'

'You've no doubt they're guilty?'

'They were practically caught in the act. Of course they're guilty. But you're asking a tiger to change its stripes. They can't help being what they are.'

'Marne?'

'They're guilty. No doubt of it. One has even confessed.'

'Throwing all the blame on the other?' Varl grunted as Marne nodded. 'I thought so. Well?'

'My decision?' Mame looked at the two men then back at Varl. 'Death.'

'I agree.'

'What?' Edallia's fingers dug into his arm. 'You're going to kill them for stealing a few stores? Why not a good whipping and let them go as Captain Chatto suggested.'

'They die.' Varl was emphatic. 'Chatto was playing Devil's Advocate and if Marne had been weak he would have lost his command by now. In any case I have the final word. Those men die. By gunfire before the entire complement. They will know why and they will know what to expect if they refuse to accept my discipline.' To the captains he rapped, 'See to it! By noon I want to be heading for Cordelia!'

It was a world of no special merit but he had emerged near it when breaking out of limbo and a ship from it had rescued him after the battle with the first alien vessel.

An act of mercy that had saved his life at the cost of endless nightmares. One that now gave him the opportunity of revenge.

He savoured it as he sat at the controls looking at the featureless swirl of limbo. One on which scenes merged one into the other; broken cities, pulped and mangled bodies, wanton destruction graced with glowing colours. Over the images another was portrayed; a face he would never forget but which he wished he could stop remembering.

'Take over Canale!'

Varl rose from his chair and strode from the control room, impatient to be moving, eager to lose his ghosts. In the engine room Roderigo smiled and made the signal that all was well. Zuber was busy with his recordings, running and rerunning them through his machine. Burchard was playing with a laser as he sat, eyes on his tell-tales.

'Just a trick, Commander.' He held out the weapon. 'I've adapted it to fit within a sleeve — see? The release is hard against a muscle and when you point your hand and flex it so it fires.' He chuckled as he demonstrated. 'The aim isn't good and the range is short but it's a handy thing to have around in certain circumstances.

Like me to make you a couple?'

'I don't want stuff like that loose among the crew.'

'You can't blame people wanting to protect themselves.'

'There are other ways. A thing like that is too tempting to use. It could go off by accident — how would you feel if you were cuddling your girl and you burned her face off.'

'Not good at all,' admitted Burchard. 'I get your point.' He threw down the adapted laser and yawned. 'I'm getting bored. Maybe I'll run a few drills.'

In the operations room Edallia put down the book she was reading as Varl entered. It was one dealing with slavery.

'I picked it up on Franzel,' she said. 'After you told me about Kendrick. A pity Ian isn't with us; he would have been able to explain.'

'Maybe.' Sabatova had returned with Edallia on the *Egon* and had joined Marne's crew. 'But I doubt it. All he would know are the same stories as we do.' Varl picked up the book, hefted it, set it down with a shrug. 'I've always wondered how some people can use so many words to explain something so simple.'

'The author goes into the psychological implications and the inherent dangers of a slavocracy.'

'Does he explain the root cause? I don't mean the sado-power complex — that kept slavery going long after the need for it had ended — but the main, basic motivation.' Varl paused then, as she looked blank, said, 'Imagine you're a landowner. You can grow all the food you can use and more beside, the only trouble is there just aren't enough hours in the day for you to do it. You need help — what do you do?'

'Hire it.'

'If it's around, maybe. But you've got no money. That comes from profit and you can't get that until you sell and you can't sell until you grow. Well?'

'I'd take in someone. Feed him, clothe him, house him.'

'And?' Varl waited. 'He's free, remember? Why should he work for just bed and board? You've got to give him more. A share of the crop, perhaps. A stake in the land. Hire too many on those terms and you'd wind up working for them.'

'So?'

'The most expensive piece of equipment around is a grown adult. Think about it. For the first dozen or so years a child needs to be fed, watched, clothed, housed, healed when it's sick, disciplined when it's bad. Fifteen years, maybe, of continuous output before it's strong enough to work in the fields. Twenty before it learns how to use simple tools and work without supervision. And it's more than cost, it's time. That's the basic reason for slavery. Ready-made labourers on the hoof, so to speak, and for those who supplied them a quick profit.'

'Economics,' Edallia sounded disappointed. 'You boil it down to greed.'

'What else? When the primitive war parties went raiding what did they hope to find? Some cloth, maybe, a few weapons, a little jewellery, some stored food — what the hell else was there? The captives provided the real loot. Fully grown industrial units ready to be used on the land, in the shipyards, as sweepers,

153

servants, metal-workers. Machines to be used then thrown away.' Varl paced the cabin. 'When they first grew sugar in the Caribbean they needed workers and fast. They bought them from the slave-traders in Africa. They worked them to death; if they got three years from a prime adult they figured it was a good deal. Economics — there's your answer.'

'There has to be more.' Edallia reached for the book. 'What about the slave-families?'

'Economics again. The price climbed so high for new stock the planters had no choice but to breed their own. Once they took that road it led them to ruin. The cost in time and consumables was simply too high for the gain received. It made better sense to free them, pay them a small wage — then charge the earth for housing, food and the rest of it. Remember the peons, the serfs, the others who worked all their lives and never once got out of debt. That's slavery too, you know. The worst kind, maybe. There are more ways to break a man's spirit than with a whip.'

'Yes.' She was firm. 'There's no real comparison. While you can walk away from something you're not a slave. Not like that poor devil you found. I'll never forget the way he cringed.'

Nor forget the way she had felt when he had. The obeisance had touched something within her. Woken an unsuspected desire. To own a slave was to be something a little more than human. To be something closer to a god.

She said impatiently, 'we could talk around it forever. How does it affect the situation?'

'Remember what I said about slave-owners needing a continual source of supply? They may have found it.'

'But — '

'I know.' Varl cut her short. 'The killing makes no sense, but think about it. They saw people, thousands of them, all gathered for easy taking. Maybe they just couldn't believe it. There had to be a catch and they tried to find it. Such valuable property had to be guarded.'

'You're guessing.' Edallia frowned at the book then pushed it away with sudden decision. 'We're wasting time. Kendrick can supply all the answers.'

He was in the infirmary, slumped in a chair, his eyes blank, his face lax. Before him Doctor Madden adjusted the glow of a hypnotic-inducting mechanism, streamers of coloured light shining in attention-focusing patterns. A recorder hummed quietly at his side.

'This is taking time.' Madden gestured at the machine. 'I'm recording everything for later study and evaluation. Zuber has the records of the initial sessions and I hope he can make more sense out of them than I could.'

'Isn't he coherent?'

'That isn't the problem. It's — well, let Zuber figure it out.'

Varl said, harshly, 'I need information, not you passing the buck. You're asking the questions and you're getting the answers. Why can't you understand them?'

'Each to his own.' Madden's tone betrayed his anger. 'I'm a physician not a technician. Come to me with a broken body and I'll fix it. Hand me a puzzle and

I'm no better than you are. Kendrick is a puzzle. A paradox, even. I ask questions and get odd answers. Listen to this.' He turned to face the slumped figure in the chair his voice — taking on the bite of command. 'Kendrick! You will answer truthfully and without hesitation. Who owned you?'

'The Lady Manukian.'

'You were bought?'

'At auction.'

'Your price?'

'Eight thousand chard.'

'Your age at the time?'

A slight hesitation then Kendrick said, 'Twenty, I think. Twenty-two.'

'Ten years,' whispered Edallia, 'He's been a slave for at least that long.'

Varl said, 'Ask him about his home.'

'I was coming to that.' Madden turned again to the slumped figure. 'You are ten years of age,' he said. 'You have gone back in time and are a child again. You are standing at a window and looking out. What do you see?'

'A garden. Houses. A road. There is traffic on the road.' Kendrick's voice was high, unbroken. 'In the distance I can see water. The beach is curved and there are people on it.'

'What is the colour of the sky?'

'Blue. The clouds are white.'

'The sun?'

'Very bright and golden.'

Madden said, 'You are now fifteen years old. You are standing in the open looking at the place in which you live. Describe it.'

'The walls are of brick and the windows have glass. The roof is tiled and there is a chimney. Behind the house the ground rises to some hills. There are other houses and streets.'

'Your name?'

'Amra Kendrick.'

'Your parents?'

'My mother is Tama Kendrick and my father is an officer on a ship of the Elgan Line.' The boyish voice held pride. 'Soon he will be a captain. Captain Singh Kendrick. When he is we shall all move to a new house in Hamburg.'

'What?' Varl pushed himself forward. 'Say that again.'

'We shall all move to a new house in Hamburg. It's in Germany. That's in — '

'I know where it is.' Varl stared at the doctor. 'Is this a joke? Do you realise what he's saying?'

'Of course I do. He claims to have been born on Earth.'

'But — '

'I've no answers,' said Madden. 'I told you that. Kendrick is a puzzle. All I can give you is a mystery.'

One Zuber deepened.

'I've checked the records,' he said. 'Like you I figured Kendrick must have been a recent loss — one of the big ships which vanished or another which just dropped out of sight. We know what happened to them and it made sense — the raider could have picked him up after he'd broken through limbo. But it isn't like that. He just isn't listed on any of them.'

'A lot of men travel loose,' said Varl. 'He needn't have left a trail.'

'True, but I found one anyway. The Elgan line. It was never big and ran into trouble when a couple of its ships crashed with a total loss of all crews.'

'Kendrick's father,' said Varl. 'He must have been among them. And?'

'The early details are sketchy — a hell of a lot of ships just left and went their own way without telling anyone, but some were on regular runs and stuck to the usual routine. The *Vishna* was one of them. A ship carrying passengers and cargo to Burgess. That's a mining world.'

'So the passengers would be all men,' said Edallia. 'Unless — '

'They were all men.' Zuber answered her question. 'Some femmikins were sent out later but they didn't do those on the *Vishna* any good. It never arrived.'

'Lost,' said Varl. 'And Kendrick was on it?'

'That's right.' Zuber leaned back in his chair.

'Amra Kendrick was listed among the passengers — which makes our friend almost three hundred years old.'

13

On Cordelia messages were waiting; delivered by a courier that had scuttled on its way. Varl read them, passed them to Zuber who pursed his lips in a whistle as he scanned the data.

'So the DNA checks out. Those blobs you sent back were bodies and human. They've sent the results of the autopsies you asked for too.' He frowned as he read them. 'Of seventy-eight selected bodies fifty-three were found to be totally deficient of potassium. Somehow it had been leeched from the system. Others — ' He broke off and looked at Varl. 'No brains,' he said bleakly. 'Are they serious?'

'Just read the report.'

Zuber swallowed and obeyed. As he finished he said, 'It doesn't make sense. Bodies found leeched of potassium and others from which the brain matter had been extracted by some form of instrument thrust up the nostrils and into the cranial cavity. But how? Why? The raiders just blasted everything in sight. They didn't even land.'

'We can't be sure of that. The only recordings we have were made by ships that appeared on the scene and scared the raiders away. On the other towns they could have landed. The bodies examined were from those other towns.'

'How were they selected?' Zuber was, abruptly, the impatient scientist. 'How found? Together? Apart? Scattered? At the edge of the ruins? Among them? Set apart? Why didn't you ask them to be precise?'

'I did,' said Varl. 'That's a preliminary report, but I don't want to spend time waiting for greater detail. Complete your summaries and send copies to Chatto and Marne. Final briefing will be in one hour.'

The *Dalio* rose shortly after it was over, Cordelia winking into view as Varl cut the hydee to align the vessel on the target-star, vanishing as the greyness of hyperspace filled the screens.

Canale said, dryly, 'What's the chances of us ever seeing it again, Commander?'

'Your guess is as good as mine.' Varl rose from his chair. 'Take over. Keep to schedule. Cut the drive to a minimum after an hour.'

To drift at the lowest velocity possible in the vicinity of where he could have torn through back into the normal universe. A chance; if a rupture existed there could be a flow of energy from one place to the other. An etheric sub-current that could work both ways as did the flow of air in a vortex tube. If the attempt failed the fleet would rendezvous on Cordelia and try again.

Now, as always, he could only wait.

Wait and study Zuber's summary and let his mind thresh over the thousand questions it created. To doze and relieve Canale and be relieved in turn. To wander the ship and listen to the transmitted vibrations of those aboard. Drilling, sleeping, gambling, killing time.

'It's crazy.' The voice whispered from the junction of deck and bulkhead, the product of an acoustic freak. 'I got it from Naomi. Those raiders are human. Human, I tell you. How the hell did they get from where they came?'

'Bad luck, accident, it happens.' The second voice was deeper. 'Ships get lost all the time. Maybe the crew managed to survive and make the best of it. If they were mixed it wouldn't be so hard. We could do it if we landed on a habitable planet. That's if we could settle a few things first.'

'Such as?'

'Who does what and with whom. Some to work and others to watch. There would have to be some arrangement with the women — sharing or a general rota. There isn't enough for us to have one each.'

'I'd like that.' The third voice chuckled. 'A share-out and maybe we could gamble our chances. Some would be worth more than others — that Edallia, for instance, I'd bet three turns with any of the others for a crack at her. She's really something.'

'I guess the Commander would agree with you.' The first voice held a shrug. 'Well, we can't all be lucky.'

'Some of us never are.'

'Luck's what you make it.' The second

voice was firm. 'Start dreaming about what you've never had and will never get is a waste of time. Just concentrate on a few of the nice things: what you'll do with your pay, for instance. How high you'll be able to fly. Hell, with enough cash you'll be able to buy a dozen well-built blondes. Got the dice? Want a game? How about us rolling against future pay?'

Men, bored, talking as soldiers always had and always would. Varl moved on, checking with automatic reflex, finally heading back to his cabin and isolation. It did morale no good for a commander to be always peering over the shoulders of his crew.

'Sir?' A woman stood outside his door, neatly rounded, nicely featured, her dark hair bearing an attractive sheen. Sylvia Kiouza who stepped closer to him as her eyes searched his face. 'Could I do anything for you, Commander?'

'Aren't you supposed to be working with Doctor Madden?'

'The infirmary isn't busy. There's nothing more I can do there. I thought I could be of more use elsewhere.' She added, 'I'm good at easing tension.'

'I guess you are.' Varl smiled at her and said, 'Kendrick is in the infirmary. Why don't you help him?'

'Amra? I — ' She broke off, looking a little abashed. 'It's not that I don't like him, but I'd rather not be with him too long. He's nice and polite but, well, he's different.'

'How?'

'I'm a woman and I know men like to be the boss. He doesn't. Some men are like that, they want to be dominated, but with Amra it's more than that. He — ' Again she broke off, shrugging helplessly. 'I can't explain it. If you were a woman you'd understand.'

'He's had a bad time,' said Varl. 'All I want you to do is to talk to him. Get him to accept you as a companion and not as a threat. Leave sex out of it. Get him to talk about his childhood, things like that. Don't demand anything. If he makes a suggestion try to follow it without making it obvious you're trying. I guess I'm asking you to teach him to be a man again.'

'It's important?'

'More than that.' Varl held her eyes. 'He's the only real guide we have to where we're going.'

The truth; information had been dug out of Kendrick scrap by scrap but he would only answer the questions he was asked. It wasn't enough. He had worked with the raiders, knew how they operated, how they ran their lives. He had to know about their cities and homes and industries. Knowledge locked behind a barrier of fear — maybe Kiouza could find the key.

Inside the cabin Edallia glared at him from where she lay sprawled on his bunk.

'I heard,' she snapped. 'That bitch offering to ease your tension. So generous of her — I guess she sensed you were itching for a change. Well, if you want her have her, but if you do you say goodbye to me!'

'What do you want?'

'I came to keep you company. To talk. I thought you'd like to have me around. Now — to hell with you!'

'You're jealous.' He stood looking down

at her. 'It makes you ugly.'

'Bastard!'

'Get out!'

He reached down as she made no move to obey, gripping her arm and dragging her to her feet. A thrust and she was outside the cabin. He slammed the door in her face.

Whiskey stood beside the cot and he drank from the bottle, sitting on the bed, feeling the warmth left by her body. A warrior-queen of ancient legend. Riding with a stallion between her thighs and a sword in her hand. Lips and teeth stained with blood from a recent kill and her blonde hair streaming in the wind. Naked flesh adorned with metal. The basic ingredient of masculine dreams.

As Sylvia Kiouza was another. The warm, dark, comforting mother-image. The home-maker. The consoler. The yielding, accommodating companion of the night who presented no threat and no challenge.

Two faces of a coin — once he'd had them combined in one.

Erica now dead. How long did she have to wait for revenge?

Varl drank again and moved to the bridge taking his place of command as he checked the panel. Touching a button he said, 'Roderigo! Change the polarity of the peap.'

'Change? But — '

'Do it!'

A moment and the *Dalio* became filled with ghosts.

They were everywhere; an invisible, bustling, jostling crowd of individual spirits. Emanations from the machine and giving the impression of real people. Bait that had once attracted horrors and Canale turned in his chair, eyes startled as he made his protest.

'For God's sake, Commander. What are you doing?'

'Watch your panel!'

'But — '

'Damn you, do as I say!' Varl flared his anger. 'How often must I repeat an order? I want immediate obedience — if you can't give it to me then stand down and I'll replace you with someone who can.'

Koslenko said, 'Nothing on the scanners, Commander.'

A trite comment and Varl knew the man had spoken only to ease the tension. Providing a shield for Canale who sat glowering at his board. A man hurt in his pride — to hell with him. He, the others, the scum from a diseased world, Varl himself, all were expendable. The reason why Kalif had given him a free hand.

'I'm taking a short-cut,' said Varl abruptly. He spoke to all in the control room but looked only at the screens. 'We could drift for weeks and get nowhere. We could try breaking through and waste power and time. If I can attract the thing that attacked the *Odile* it might be possible to create the same conditions. It must fashion a strain of some kind. Maybe it tears its way through from beyond.'

Canale said, 'We had a plan. The others — '

'Could be drawn through the opening if we make one.'

'I was thinking of the risk.'

'That'll be all ours.' Segman knew of the danger. 'They aren't radiating what we are.'

The ghost-crowd that gave the illusion of the *Dalio* carrying a far greater number than she did. But they were safe. The living crew was not.

A gamble and Varl sweated as he waited it out. To reverse polarity now and try to make the break? To wait until the thing had closed in? How long would it be?

Touching the intercom Varl said, 'On-duty watch take action-alert.' A compromise, one discarded as soon as made. Now there could be no half-measures. 'Correction. Cancel the last. All crew on battle alert!'

Waiting, suited, nursing instruments of destruction. Nerves as tense as violin strings as, in the control room, Varl juggled with their lives.

He waited too long.

Edallia saw it first; a glint in the air which swelled to form a sphere, a cylinder, a polyhedron. Shrinking to a point again as it winked out to reappear at a battle-station where men stood ready to feed torpedoes into the maw of launchers.

A thin lance of silver brilliance drifting

to touch a suited figure.

To turn it into a ghastly parody of the human shape.

The suit vanished, replaced by oozing flesh and the stark whiteness of bone, the bloated shapes of distorted organs. The legs shortened, the feet wreathed by ropes of steaming intestines. The heart beat where the stomach should have been and the eyes rested like veined marbles in the palms of blunted hands.

From the twisted gap of a mouth that ran where the spine should have been came a keening whine.

One that died as, abruptly, the distorted thing shrank and vanished.

'Freeze!' Varl shouted over the intercom. 'Don't move! Roderigo! Reverse the polarity and stand by for cascade!'

The ghosts vanished, replaced by the familiar deadness as even the life-emanations of the crew were nullified by the peap. At his station Varl watched the dials, the read-outs, checking the entire bank of instruments as power flooded into the hydee. More power than it normally held. A river of energy that flooded the balanced coils and threatened the stability of the entire unit.

But only threatened. Once it had been a matter of luck; now the technicians had provided safeguards.

'Near cascade-level.' Roderigo reported from the engine room. 'When — '

A scream and he was silent. Varl watched his board, sweating, cursing his mistake. Power should have been fed into the hydee when the peap had been reversed. The cascade ready to trip and everything ready to go. He had waited too long and crew had died. Roderigo? Burchard? Edallia? Any of the others who had trusted him with their lives?

'Commander!' Koslenko gestured at his panel. 'I think there's something out there.'

'All guns open fire!'

Varl felt the ship tremble beneath him as the order was obeyed. Wasted munitions; the fourth-dimensional thing which attacked them was proof against their fury, but action would maintain the morale of the crew.

'Cascade ready!' Roderigo's voice — the

scream had not been his. 'Commander?'

'Who died?'

'God knows. I heard the scream and froze. The cascade?'

'I'll handle it.' Varl hit another button. 'All stations cease fire! Cease fire!' He paused, counting. 'Here we go!'

He tripped the cascade.

Energy flooded into the hydee, pushing it past the edge of tolerance, radiating out to embrace the entire vessel in a wave of irresistible force. One that could only run from limbo and never back into normal space. A pulse that could only go one way.

Like a pip squeezed from between a finger and thumb the *Dalio* spurted from where it rested.

Into another universe.

14

A riot of colour shone where there should have been the empty darkness of normal space; brilliant greens, reds, blues, yellows. Orange, puce, violet, the hard whiteness of eternal ice, the warm browns of autumn leaves.

A plethora of variegated hues and, amongst them, drifted objects; pyramids, cones, spires, cubes, spheres of different shades, polyhedrons, things like snowflakes, others like sponges.

An alien universe Varl had seen before.

'We made it.' He said into the intercom: 'Maintain battle-alert.' To Koslenko he said, 'Any sign of the other ships?'

'No.' The man checked his scanners. 'But there's something moving towards us on the upper-port side. One of those pyramids.'

'Veer away. Use rockets.' Varl snarled his impatience as Canale was slow to obey. 'I'll take over. Go and check the ship.'

It trembled beneath his hands as Varl fired the rockets. A touch that sent streamers of flame stabbing into the void. Another and their velocity was negated relative to where they had emerged.

'Koslenko?'

'Clear now. Still no sign of the others.' He added, 'Should we radio? A sharp signal to let them know we're here?'

'It would attract what attacked us. We'll wait.'

Time in which to remove the suits and ease aching muscles. To change watches and check the ship for damage.

Canale was bitter. 'Two men dead and for what? Because you couldn't wait. We had a plan and you jumped it. The others could all be dead now. Ripped apart by that thing you attracted. Turned inside out like Denton and Vogel and left with their guts trailing the deck.'

Segman said, uneasily, 'Take it easy, Max.'

'It's the truth, isn't it? We broke through so they paid the price. Someone always pays the price.'

From his board Koslenko said, 'Still no sign, Commander.'

Ignoring him Varl stared at the first officer.

'You don't like me and you don't like taking my orders, right? Well, mister, you were warned. Stand down and report for normal crew-duties. I've another to take your place,'

'You can't do that.' Canale glanced at the others then met Varl's eyes. 'I'm under direct orders from the Comptroller. He assigned me to be your second in command. To take over in case of need. I figure that time is now.'

'You're lying.'

'You think so?' Canale fumbled in a pocket. 'I've his signed order. It entitles me to take over the ship. I'm doing just that.'

'Like hell you are!'

Varl lunged forward as the officer's hand appeared, his own slamming out, the fist smashing against the bicep, paralysing it, the arm, the fingers holding the laser. As it fell to the deck he struck again, a savage, vicious blow with the stiffened edge of his palm. Canale's neck snapped with the sound of breaking wood. As he fell light and noise blared from Koslenko's panel.

'Metal,' he reported. 'Something big coming at us and fast.' His voice rose as he checked his instruments. 'A ship! Commander, it's a ship!'

The *Keil* and it was a wreck.

Varl guided the *Dalio* towards it, matching velocities, studying the vessel as it came close. The hull was indented, scarred as if by tremendous claws. Turrets had been ripped open, the guns they contained turned into masses of twisted and fused rubbish. From a gaping rent in the hull suited figures drifted on the ends of safety lines.

A dozen of them — less than a third of the crew.

Chatto was among them. He sat in a chair in the operations room, a drink in his hand, blood staining one cheek and the fingers of his left hand. A man trembling with mental and physical exhaustion.

'Here.' Madden handed him a pill.

'This will give you a boost. Wash it down with that whiskey.' To Varl he said, 'I can use some more help in the infirmary.'

'Pick who you want. Get those people back in shape as fast as you can.'

Eight men, four women, three with broken limbs which inset metal-splints would quickly make useable. Three with internal injuries, all with bruises and contusions.

'It happened too fast,' said Chatto. The pill and drink had cured his trembling. 'I tried following the plan but it got us nowhere. Then I took a chance and reversed the peap.' He looked at Varl, at Edallia and Burchard who sat listening. 'Crazy, maybe, but what else could I do? Then things went crazy. The ship was thrown to hell and gone. I tried firing. I even tried cutting the hydee. Then, suddenly, I was where you found us.'

In a dead ship with a three-parts dead crew and extinction staring him in the face.

Varl refilled his glass and said, 'Did you see anything of the *Egon*?'

'No.'

Marne would have played it by the

book and, if so, the chances were high he would be safe. Reversing the peap seemed essential in order to break through limbo. Or, more exactly, the influence of the thing it attracted was critical.

'You were right,' said Burchard. 'It was the only way to get through. Canale was wrong.'

'Canale?' Chatto lowered his glass. 'Your first officer?'

'He was.' Varl was curt. 'He's gone now. The job's yours if you want it.'

Back in the control room Varl slumped into his chair and stared at the screens. Edallia had accompanied him to squat at his side.

Quietly she said, 'I heard what happened. Did you have to kill him?'

'He had a gun. He wanted to use it.'

'So you executed him for mutiny. Was he Kalif's agent?' She answered her own question. 'It's possible and I'll bet there's more than one. That's if they're still alive. Most of the regulars Chatto carried are dead. More died when you downed the raider. If any of his spies are left they'll be keeping their heads down.' She added,

'Still angry with me?'

'No.'

'Then — '

'Let's forget it for now.' He gestured at the screens. 'What impression does that give you?'

'Paint.' She thought a moment. 'Some fluid with bits in. Soup or — '

'Blood?'

'Maybe.' She frowned, thinking. 'Those objects could be platelets, corpuscles, antibodies — if so they could be dangerous.'

'They are. Get too close and they can change and attack. Drifting with them and staying clear we're fairly safe. It's as if we were in a current,' he explained. 'One leading to a common node. Everything breaking through limbo into the Drift winds up there.'

'The Drift?'

'What you see. Zuber called it that.'

Edallia looked at the shapes limned in the screens, the colours. She remembered the scientist's explanations; rough attempts to make the inexplicable understandable by the use of crude analogies. Limbo — the skin surrounding the normal universe. The rind of an orange which, broken, led to this alien region. Or to the central pith of the fruit via some bizarre dimension. A place that led all entering it to a common point. Like rain falling from the sky, dripping from roofs, to be fed down gutters, pipes, finally to be guided into the ocean.

'It scares me,' she said.

'You'll get used to it.'

'It's all right for you — you've been here before.'

'So has Kendrick.' Varl rose from his chair. 'Let's see what he can tell us.'

He had changed since being found. There was strength to him that had been lacking; a braver set to his shoulders, a prouder lift to his head. Koiuza's work together with Madden's therapy. That coupled with the demonstration of equality between men and women — on the *Dalio* there were no slaves.

'You've been here before.' Varl gestured at the monitor screens in the operations room. 'In the *Vishna*. Can you tell us anything about it?'

'I've told Jac all I know.' Kendrick

made a small, helpless gesture. 'It wasn't much. It was a long time ago.'

Two hundred and fifty-three years. After his father had died economic necessity had forced the boy to find work in the African mines. Hard, unremitting labour which had left its mark. Later, trained, he had headed for Burges. He had been a slave for ten years.

What had happened in between?

'We were cramped,' said Kendrick. 'Passage was cheap but conditions were rough. They kept us in the cabins and fed us slop and we had to share beds. None of us got a chance to see outside and, after a while, we began to get worried. The journey was lasting too long,' he explained. 'There had been a lot of jerking around and some of us were hurt. One had died.'

'And then?'

'The crew let us move around in the hold.' Kendrick glanced at Edallia. 'One of them seemed to like me and hinted something was wrong. He talked about a crazy place full of broken rainbows. The hydee had broken and we could do nothing but drift.'

Varl said, 'For how long?'

'I don't know. The rations were cut and cut again. Water was short and the air began to go bad. Most of us just flopped around and slept. I was lucky, I guess. My friend took me up to his cabin. I didn't get to see outside but I did get better food and the air wasn't as bad. Then — well, I just don't know.'

The answer he had given Zuber but Varl probed deeper.

'Think,' he urged. 'You were feeling doped, ill, but you must have known what was happening. Seen something odd.'

'No, I don't think so.'

'Your friend,' said Edallia. 'Did you notice anything unusual about him?'

'He'd slowed down.' Kendrick nodded as he thought about it. 'He used to have a trick. He'd balance something on the back of his hand, turn it, catch what it was before it hit the floor. After a while he couldn't do that. He missed every time. And the clock.' He frowned as he dredged his memory. 'The bad air must have affected our minds. I slept a lot and the hands seemed to be moving too fast. It was an old fashioned clock,' he explained. 'My friend liked to watch the jerk of the second hand. It got so that I couldn't even see it.'

'Let's move on,' said Varl. 'To when you were rescued.'

'I don't remember it.'

'Nothing about it at all?'

'I must have fallen into a coma or something. The next thing I knew was being in a pen with some of the others. We were washed, fed and exercised. Later we were led into a compound to be inspected. From there we were sold.'

'Who did the washing and feeding?' Edallia asked the question. 'Men or women?'

'Men. They wore collars.'

Thick metal bands as unlike the one he had worn as a bracelet was to a manacle. Low-value property put to do the dirty work. Then the inspection when they had been checked and prodded like cattle. Then the sale. One like others she had known on decadent worlds where men and women offered themselves at public auction. But they only sold their temporary services — for Kendrick it had been for life.

Had his buyer got her money's worth?

'Slowing down,' said Varl after Kendrick had left them. 'Did you get it? The apparent speed of falling objects, the acceleration of the clock? He put it down to the bad air but there could be another explanation.'

'An actual change in his body-metabolism.' She nodded, thoughtfully. 'That or time-distortion. The longer they drifted the more they slowed down. When they reached the node then, maybe — '

'Stasis.' Varl was ahead of her. 'The ship stopped. Everything stopped. The hands of the clock, the air-circulators, everything. But before that the crew and passengers would have slipped into a state of suspended animation. Every bodily function would have slowed and, at the end, frozen in stasis.'

Edallia said, 'It accounts for Amra being so old. He just rested there for two and a half centuries and it could have been ten times that if he hadn't been rescued. For eternity, even. Varl! Do you realise what this means?'

Every ship that had ever entered the Drift from the beginning of time could be waiting at the central node. The secrets they contained, the crews they had carried. Vessels that had vanished loaded with valuable cargoes. Others thought to have been destroyed.

Among them could be Kreutzal's ship — the *Lieber*. The ship and the man himself still, possibly, alive.

15

Salan Chatto was medium-built, middle-aged, his skin swarthy, his eyes deep-set, cold. A man who knew when to laugh and joke and when to be icy hard. One who had adopted battle as a profession; a mercenary who had run his own ship during the Venegian war. Then he had been on the losing side.

'I've been doing some figuring, Kurt.' He sat in Canale's place, recovered now, slipping into the *Dalio's* routine like a hand into a glove. 'According to Kendrick the *Vishna* ran out of food and water and the air went bad. Admitting the crew was probably holding back on supplies that still takes time. A lot of time; the circulators would have kept the air viable if nothing else.'

'So how long did they drift? Is that it?'

Chatto nodded.

Varl said, 'There's no way of telling. A long time, sure, but how long is anyone's guess. Things have improved since then and we can't tell how far they entered the Drift from the central node. Nor how they travelled. 'They could have spiralled in,' he explained. 'My guess is that they did.'

'Why?'

'They survived.' Varl narrowed his eyes at the screen, at the objects close around them. One was too close and he snapped to the navigator: 'Segman! Watch it! That thing to port!'

'It wasn't there a second ago.' Segman checked his panel. 'Our course is unchanged.'

'Koslenko?'

From the scanners he said, 'It jumped. It was a pyramid before. Now it's changed.'

Into a clustered mass of jutting spears. Protrusions which altered as they watched, becoming writhing tentacles edged with jagged teeth.

'Two more objects approaching from the rear,' said Koslenko. 'Large and moving fast.'

And another like a bulbous sponge moving before them. The attack Varl had feared. His hand reached for the intercom.

'Battle alert! Man all stations!'

Burchard said, 'Report when settled. Radio — '

'No radio!' Varl drowned out the voice from the speaker. 'Communicate by wire-relay only. Roderigo! Boost peap to full reverse polarity. Stand by for rocket power.' He waited, counting seconds as the machine of his command swung into lethal preparedness. 'Stand ready to fire.'

Chatto said, 'Why not use hydee and run for it?'

'Too dangerous. Remember what happened to the *Keil*?'

'Here? Now?'

'It could happen. Koslenko?'

'More moving in from starboard up and down. A squeeze play, Commander.'

One begun as a writhing tentacle lashed against the ship filling the interior with the drumming echoes from its beaten hull. Thunder repeated as warning lights flashed on the instrument panels.

'Laser guns port side! Burn that thing!'

Varl reached for the controls as the gunners obeyed. Livid fire spurted from the tentacles that twitched as if seared with molten metal. A portion of one broke free to swirl, to become a glinting spear, a whirling pyramid. One that darted away as again the tentacles lashed at the *Dalio*.

'Torps!'

In an emergency Varl could fire the fixed weaponry from the control room but it was better handled from fire-control. And he had other duties. As power fed the rockets he felt the ship jerked like a goaded horse, to hurtle towards the amorphous mass waiting before them. One which seemed to expand as they approached, to burst into a hundred fragments as the torpedoes slammed out to vent their fury in blasts of searing destruction.

'We're clear.' Koslenko echoed his relief. 'We've left them all behind.'

But others waited ahead and to either side. They moved in, triggered by some unknown signal, the very matter of this alien place responding to the threat of an invader.

'Burchard?'

'All under control. We can blast

anything that comes at us.' He added, grimly, 'As long as we've the tools to do it with.'

'Hold all fire.'

The signal could be local and speed would carry them away from the threat. Too high a velocity could create its own hazard but to simply drift would take too much time. Men had starved on the *Vishna*. Gone mad, died — that would not happen in the *Dalio*.

'Koslenko. Check all objects.' Varl adjusted the thrusting blast of the rockets. 'Are those ahead closing in towards us?'

A moment then Koslenko said, 'Slowly, yes.'

'Segman?'

'We can change course to miss the main body of them.' The navigator checked his calculations. 'Slow down a tenth, Commander. Another two percent. That's it.' Again his fingers danced over the keys of his computer. 'Change course fifteen degrees port in fifty-eight seconds. Hold for eleven. Return to original course plus nine degrees.'

A zigzag that sent the *Dalio* slipping

between the massed threats. Twice they had to blast objects from their path then the ship was hurtling smoothly on its way.

'That should do it.' Varl cut the drive and reached for the intercom. 'Stand down from battle alert. Standard watch only.'

Chatto said, 'Gambling, Commander?'

'Saving our strength. You know what happens when crews are kept on full alert too long.'

'They don't like it. They lose their edge, itch, get restless, fall into a trance-state. I've known guards on watch just sit staring while men walked up and killed them. They didn't even recognise their danger.' Chatto added, meaningfully, 'The same applies to officers.'

'Which is why you can earn your keep.' Varl rose, stretched, looked down at the other. 'Take over. Have Koslenko and Segman relieved; one after the other at a two-hour interval.'

He left the control room and checked the ship. All was as it should be; the crew exhilarated by the recent action. Edallia was waiting in his cabin.

She said, 'If you throw me out this time I'll kill you. I swear it.'

'Didn't we make peace?'

'We talked,' she corrected. 'You said you weren't angry with me. You didn't say you wanted to share a drink and get close. Do you?'

'I'll have the drink,' he said. 'I'll even sit beside you. What did you want to talk about?'

'Did I say I wanted to talk?'

She leaned towards him, lips parted and he could smell the whiskey on her breath. Catch, too, the odour of ka'sence that hung about her nostrils and the golden sheen of her hair. The mounds of her breasts thrust against the fabric of her blouse accentuating her femininity as did the swell of her hips, the long lines of her thighs.

A woman reacting from recent strain. Stimulated by danger, action, the threat of destruction. Urged by nature to fulfil her natural function.

'Kurt, damn you! You know — '

'Where's that drink?' He took it, sipped, waved aside the small box she proffered. 'No thanks.'

'Suit yourself.' She opened it, took out a pod, crushed it between finger and thumb and inhaled the released vapours. The scent of ka'sence drowned the acrid odour of the spirit, tainting it so that Varl downed the whiskey no longer liking its taste. 'Here!' She refilled his glass.

'Now kiss me.'

The kiss led to a touch, to a caress, to a sudden fire that burned away all restraint. Later, lying naked on the bed, Edallia turned to stare at him in his matching nudity.

'I love you,' she said abruptly. 'Kurt, I love you. I've never said that to any man before and meant it, 'but this time I do.'

He made no answer and she felt the tiny twitch of muscles in her forearm, the tension of fingers that curved as if with a life of their own.

'Kurt?'

'I heard you.'

She moved, lifting herself on one arm to look down at his face and body. A hard face, leached of passion now, emotionless as if carved from stone. One that matched the body with its broad shoulders and narrow waist. The arms that had held her so tightly now rested lax at his sides and she ran her fingers over them, making small traceries that moved to his chest, his stomach.

'I love you, Kurt. Don't you understand?'

'So you love me.' He sat upright and reached for the bottle and drank from it some of the whiskey running down his chin. 'Now I know.'

'Don't you care?'

'Should I?' He turned towards her. 'What you really want is for me to tell you I'm in love with you too.'

'Don't you?'

'Does it matter?' His eyes held hers. 'You wanted, you had, why make a big thing about it?'

'Damn you!' Anger roughened her voice. 'You make it seem as if I just wanted you to scratch an itch.' His shrug fuelled her rage. 'If that was all I wanted I could have had any man in the ship. They'd have come running. And they would have been grateful.'

'And told you they loved you and whispered all sorts of sweet lies and promised the earth just so they could get back again.' Varl swung his legs over the edge of the bed and stood looking down at her. 'That's what you really want — a man at your feet.'

One of whom she could be proud. A man who would put her wishes before the urgency of his lust. Who would do what she wanted without her having to ask. One who would acknowledge her superiority.

In Varl she thought she had found such a man but now she realised her mistake. The very qualities that made him so attractive worked against him ever being subservient to her or anyone else.

'You don't love me,' said Varl. 'I don't believe you know what love is. To you the word is part of a game. A thing to use like another would offer a bribe or use a fist. Something to help you get your own way.'

She said, bitterly, 'You could have lied. At least you could have given me that.'

'I love you.' He dropped to his knees before her. 'I love the touch of your skin, the scent of your hair, the soft warmth of your lips. For me your body holds all a man could ever hope to gain. Your words are music. Your embrace is paradise. I love you, darling. I love you.' Words without meaning, as devoid of emotion as was his face, his eyes. Without change of tone he added, 'You see? Words to play a game we are both good at. No.' His hand rose to touch the golden sheen of her hair. 'That wasn't true. It's a game I can't play. I'm not clever enough.'

But cunning enough to be aware of the danger of a woman scorned. And reluctant to admit to weakness — no man in love could ever be truly strong. Things she realised as she knew he had salvaged her pride.

'Kurt!' Her hand moved to touch him and she felt her response as her fingers touched his flesh. A warm flow of mounting desire that sent her arms to clasp his thighs against her breasts. 'Kurt! I love you, darling! I love you!' A game she could play. One she would win. 'Please, darling, I need you. Kurt — ' She snarled her anger as someone pounded

198

on the cabin door. 'Damn! Who the hell's that?'

It was Zuber. His eyes widened a little at the sight of Varl and Edallia on the bed.

'Sorry, Commander, but Chatto sent me to tell you.'

'About what?'

'The central node. We've reached it.' Zuber's voice rose as Varl made no reply. 'Kurt! Don't you get it! We've arrived!'

16

There was majesty to it and a stately grandeur as if time and space had conjoined to create a smoothly functioning machine. One filled with colour and movement that shone from the screens. An image that held a teasing familiarity.

Edallia named it. 'Saturn. It looks like Saturn.'

A dully glowing ball surrounded with diverse rings which sparkled and flashed in winking shards of transient brilliance. Haloes composed of myriads of assorted shapes and sizes. Fragments and massive lumps mixed with items of smaller dimension all locked together in the wheeling measure of an eternal saraband.

'A closed system,' said Zuber. 'It has to be. Everything breaking into the Drift is swept towards it and spiralled into orbit. The central core has mass and therefore a gravitational pull. My guess is that it radiates a repelling force of some kind to prevent the trapped matter falling to its surface.'

Chatto said, 'Would that be the same force which froze the *Vishna*?'

'Most probably.' Zuber frowned at the image, trying to make out smaller detail. 'Can this be enlarged?'

For answer Varl touched a control. On the screens the image widened as electronic magnification worked its magic. It steadied, settled as the maximum amplification was reached.

'Ships!' Edallia sucked in her breath. 'They're ships!'

Three of them, old-fashioned in construction, one with its hull ripped open from bow to stern, another coated with an ebon layer blotched with craters. The third, apparently unharmed, bore faded markings.

'The *Tremaine*? *Tremeron*?' Edallia shook her head. 'I can't make it out.'

'If it's the *Tamerlaine* it could be worth going after.'

Chatto narrowed his eyes. 'She vanished with a cargo of diamond-tipped drills. A fortune on any mining world.'

Edallia said, 'There could be others. Can't we get closer?'

'We're doing that all the time,' reminded Varl. 'Too close and we might be in trouble.'

'The stasis?' Zuber thought he understood. 'I think we're safe until we begin to spiral towards the core. The effects this far out can only be small.'

Varl was thinking of something else; of the raiders who could even now be searching the trapped vessels for their frozen crews. He diminished the image and looked at the alien shapes that had thickened around them. Objects apparently immune to the pull of the central mass.

His hand reached for the intercom.

'Stand by for flight. Get up here, Segman. You too Koslenko. All crew on standby alert.' He looked at Edallia. 'That means you. You too, Jac.'

The reliefs accompanied them as they left the bridge.

Segman grunted as he took his station. Koslenko checked his scanners.

'Nothing but our usual friends. You

want to run from them, Commander?'

'Not until we have to. Keep us straight, Segman. I don't want to get into a spiral course.'

'I'll watch it.' The navigator worked at his panel. 'Edging to port.'

'Much?'

'A half degree.' He added, 'I'll give course-correction when it doubles that and accelerates.'

Fifteen minutes later Chatto said, sharply, 'What's that?'

Flickers like darting sparks rising from one side of the massed and wheeling debris.

'Koslenko?'

'Fast movement to starboard, Commander. I can't determine the mass.'

'Numbers?'

'Two to a dozen or more. There's no way of telling. All I register is rapid but intermittent movement.'

'Battle-stations!' Varl sounded the alarm. 'All crew on battle alert!' He waited, giving the crew time to don suits, struggling into his own, sitting again with the face plate open. Ramming the communication-wire into its socket he said, 'We move on five. Mark!'

The rockets were safe but slow and would betray their position. The hydee could attract unwanted attention from the thing that had already taken two lives and had wrecked the *Keil* but using it was the only way to move quickly from the alien shapes and the raiders who could have spotted them.

Varl tensed as the screens blurred, clearing to show the central core close and below.

The raiders that were his target.

They flitted like gnats, bizarre, oddly beautiful, hulls shimmering with gold. Three of them busy at their search with another two drifting close to vessels locked in the outer bands.

'Fire!' Varl slammed shut his faceplate. 'All units open fire!'

An attack without warning, surprise their main weapon, one that sent two of the raiders into incandescent ruin as unleashed torpedoes blasted through their hulls. The gold of the others turned to green, back to gold again as lavender fury tore at the *Dalio*.

Varl felt the shudder as one hit, heard the scream, then the screens flickered as he engaged the interrupter and he was firing in turn.

A matter of synchronisation; to fire while their defences were down and to withstand their own attack while doing so. One ship he could handle, more needed the lightning-swift reflexes of computers. The *Dalio* jerked to the stat of electronic impulses, shook to the release of torpedoes that burst in ravening gouts of blue-white.

Not all were wasted. A raider showed a broken hull, a smear of darkness against the gold. A hit followed by others as torpedoes and laser guns blasted the damaged vessel. It spun, lavender fire streaming from bow and stern, exploding in a sudden eruption of debris and flame.

Air blasted from the control room as a jagged fragment ripped through the hull.

'There's more of them,' said Chatto. 'Rising from the wrecks.'

'Take over! Evasive action!' Varl chinned the intercom switch as the other obeyed.

A man could only concentrate on one thing at a time. 'Sections in turn, report on damage.'

They had been lucky but it was bad enough; three turrets ruined, a compartment wrecked and three others open to space. Men and women dead, hurt or dying, lying where they had fallen.

'We're outnumbered,' said Chatto. 'Beaten. Those damned screens! We have to run.'

Scuttling into hyperspace. To emerge to face the fury of lavender beams. To run again.

'They can trail us.' Chatto twisted in his chair. 'Commander?'

'Keep dodging. Roderigo? Start the cascade.'

Prepare the energy that would kick them back into their own sane, normal universe. Beaten, retreating, but living to fight another day. A mercenary's reaction but one Varl shared. The *Dalio* wasn't strong enough. No ship would be until a real defence was found. A screen like that used by the raiders,

'Roderigo?'

'Level rising. In — ' Varl heard the sudden intake of the engineer's breath. God! Dear God, no!'

'What is it? Roderigo? Answer man!'

'It's back! That thing. It — no! No!'

A glint, a shape in the air, one that changed with bewildering complexity. The probing finger of a curious four-dimensional being or the ravening claw of a mindless beast — the result would be the same. A human body turned into something obscene. Tormented, distorted, left to whimper and mew in tongueless agony.

'Roderigo!' Varl hit another switch. 'All personnel — freeze! Don't move! Don't communicate!'

Sit crouched like the dead and hope immobility would buy safety. Let the glinting destruction rove as it would for nothing could stop it. Just wait until the cascade was ready to trip and the nightmare could be ended.

'Roderigo?' Varl waited. 'Roderigo? Can you answer?'

Silence — he could be talking to a ghost. Or a thing unable to hear, to talk, to see. And the very movement of electrons in his communicator could have put him at risk.

Varl reached forward to wipe the panel; the outrush of air had coated the instruments with a patina of frost. It yielded to his glove to reveal the level of energy in the cascade.

'Commander!' Roderigo's voice was taut with strain. 'That thing! It's probing the hydee!'

Varl hit the release.

The *Dalio* jerked, twisted, echoed to the impact of metal, the shrill of unleashed forces. Lights flared on the instrument panels, dimmed by the frost but unmistakable in their message of destruction. Air lost, bulkheads torn, a passage ripped from the engine room into space. The ship itself spinning on its short axis, tumbling, the screens no longer grey but streaked with light.

'We made it!' Varl sent fire jetting from the rockets; opposed thrusts that slowed the tumbling of the ship followed by deft touches that brought it to relative steadiness. 'We've broken through.'

'No,' said Chatto. 'All we did was get away.' He pointed at the screens. 'See it?'

A blur like a spiral nebula. One formed of colour and movement with a central core ringed like Saturn. Far distant now but the screens brought it close enough to recognise.

As they did the worlds all around. Too many worlds and all too close. Spheres like brightly painted marbles hanging in the peculiar umber haze generated by a swollen sun.

One was very close.

'We've got to land.' Segman coughed as if his lungs were filled with blood. 'The ship's a wreck.'

One needing a haven as did the crew. The hydee was useless but the rockets could get them down. Varl fired them and sent the *Dalio* towards the world pictured large in the screens. One banded with stripes that changed as they approached to become ranges of mountains, lakes, fertile areas. Spots that could have been villages. A blotch that had to be a city.

From it rose lavender fire.

'Damn them!' Varl dodged, tripped the bow, thrust the rockets to full power. 'We'll aim for the hills.'

The *Dalio* juddered as a beam struck, the stem jerking as if kicked. Air began to whine past the ripped hull as Varl flung the vessel like a flaming arrow towards the loom of hills he had spotted beyond the city. A gamble to hit the downward slopes, to skid over them, letting friction and the forward blast of the rockets negate both their velocity and the tug of gravity.

A matter of split-second timing and instant decision.

Varl tensed as the peaks of the hills came close. A blast from the bow and it lifted to clear jagged rock, lowering as he opposed the initial thrust with a stronger.

The rear venturis died and, for a long moment, the *Dalio* hung suspended in the air as the slope spun past beneath it.

'Crash alert!' Varl yelled the warning. 'Pad down for impact!'

Fire spurted from the forward vents as he applied full power to the bow rockets. The ship jerked, veered a little, straightened as he corrected then, suddenly, they were down.

To the whining shrill of rasping metal

as the hull slid over dirt and rock. To a wild confusion of sound and movement: screams, the metallic grate of yielding bulkheads, the drone of air past the ship as it plummeted towards the foothills.

To slew and spin and come to a final rest.

17

Segman was dead; the fragment that had ripped through the hull had glanced off his chest, not rupturing his suit but sending the jagged ends of broken ribs to lacerate his lungs. The crash had done the rest as it killed Murrey, Goetzer, Potts, Tate. Names to add to those killed during the battle. A list that grew as Varl roved the ship, finding those hopelessly injured, giving them mercy with relentless detachment.

Only then did he give his attention to the ship.

'It's useless.' Chatto had lived together with Zuber, Edallia, Koslenko, Madden, a score of others, the doctor now treating their wounds. 'The hydee's ruined.'

'Jac?'

'He's right.' Zuber, like them all, had doffed his suit and looked drawn, one cheek marred by an ugly bruise. 'One coil's burned out and the synchronisation of the rest must be all to hell. Even if we had spares they'd have to be tuned.'

An engineer's job, but Roderigo and his staff had been voided from the ship in the gust of escaping air. Varl looked at the ragged opening, at the smear of colour staining one edge. Blood? Brain? Bone?

He said, 'So we forget the *Dalio*. Gather up all the supplies we can carry; food, water, arms. Be heavy on the arms.'

As Chatto moved off shouting orders, Zuber said, 'What's the plan, Commander? To run off and hide in the hills? How long can we survive?'

'Longer than if we stay here.' Varl stepped from the ship and looked at the sky. The peculiar umber haze was lightened by the lowering ball of the sun. Nearby worlds looked like distant stars. 'They must have seen us from that city. They fired on us and would have tracked us down. Soon they'll come looking for us. I'd rather we weren't here when they arrive.'

'They won't stop looking.'

'The longer they do it the less dangerous we'll seem. Now they're liable to shoot on sight. If we can get away and stay hidden until the excitement dies down maybe we can do something.'

'Like enter the city, steal a ship, head back into the Drift?' Zuber looked at the nebula-like smear in the sky. 'It must be a weak-point between the universes,' he said, 'Get into it and then get kicked through. The only way we can get back home.' Shaking his head he added, 'We'd never make it.'

'Why not?' Varl didn't wait for an answer. 'There's not much else we can do. With luck they'll think we all died in the crash and stop looking. With Kendrick to guide us we night be able to work it. Now let's get loaded and on our way.'

They managed eight hundred yards.

The raider flicked into being as Varl altered course to pass a cluster of boulders; fresh dirt and broken plants telling of their recent landing. He halted, staring up at the gleaming, golden hull, hands lifted, palms empty and facing the menace. A posture adopted by the others. One held as the bizarre vessel drifted over towards the *Dalio*, rose a little, returned to land beside the column.

'Steady!' Varl gave the warning as a patch darkened the golden hull; the mouth of an opening port. 'Make no movement. Say no word.'

A warning ignored as figures stepped to the ground.

'By God!' A man called out from lower down the column. 'They're women!'

A dozen of them, tall, thick masses of hair dressed in elaborate confusion about aristocratic, blue-eyed faces. Hair as blonde as sun-ripened wheat and eyes as cold as eternal ice. Their shoulders were wide, legs long, waists narrow beneath the cincture of ornamented belts. Bright clothing of subtle composition accentuated rather than shielded the femininity of breasts, buttocks, the swell of hips. Boots reached almost to their knees. All bore guns.

Each carried a whip dangling from her wrist.

They spread to cover the column, with their guns and Varl guessed at other weapons aimed at them from the ship. To resist would invite lavender fire that would turn them all into ash.

To Chatto he whispered, 'Pass the word. No heroics. This isn't our party.'

The action had been taken from his hands and placed in those from the ship. He watched as their leader came closer to the column; a woman with clear-cut features as hard as iron. One who inspected them all with searching eyes.

'You!' She pointed at Edallia. 'Why did you bring your vessel to Gorm?'

'She isn't the captain,' said a man three places from her. 'If you want — '

He broke off as the leader moved, closing the space between them, her whip lifting, falling to slash his face above the eyes.

As he recoiled she said, to Edallia, 'I wonder you allow your chiros such licence. Now tell me why you came to Gorm.'

'You are?'

'Mirza Lamprect. Captain of the *Hagler*.' She spoke the name and rank with pride. The whip gestured at the golden hull. 'Answer me, woman!'

Edallia squared her shoulders. The

mistake had been natural; blonde herself the woman would have expected a blonde to be in command. It would never have occurred to her that anything as lowly as a man could have held that position. Armed with Kendrick's knowledge Edallia knew how she must act.

'First I demand an apology.' She was cold. 'If any chiro of mine needs punishing I will see to it. Your whip could have blinded and caused needless damage to valuable property. As for the rest — that will be explained to your superiors.'

'My orders — '

'Were to investigate the situation. I understand.'

Edallia edged her tone with impatience. 'The apology?'

A moment then, reluctantly, 'Perhaps I was hasty with the whip. I am not accustomed to insult and cannot tolerate insolence from a chiro.'

'In that we are agreed.' Edallia relaxed, smiling as she stepped towards the other woman. 'I see no reason for enmity between us. I am Edallia Kramer. Captain of the *Dalio*, which, as you see, is unfortunately a wreck. I had no choice but to land on Gorm. I was hoping to make my way to the city and am more than gratified you have come to my rescue.'

An assumption, one Lamprect accepted. 'I shall transport you and your companions to the city.' She added, with a note of envy, 'Do you always travel with so many chiros?'

A question repeated by the Lady Venicia Dobie.

She was smaller than Lamprect, older, the gold of her hair paled by incipient grey. Her femininity was less flaunted; soft fabrics moulding the contours of her body, more alluring in their suggestive drapery than the other's blatant aggression. But her eyes were as hard and her mind more agile. An instrument of her thrusting interrogation.

'So many chiros,' she murmured. 'A few ship-boys would be natural but the ones you carried were hardly that. Would you care to explain?'

Edallia took her time. It had been hours since the crash and she was beginning to ache. Becoming tired of the endless questioning, too, and more than a little irritated. She said, sharply, 'Lady, please stop acting as if you are an innocent. I carried chiros because it suited me to do so. You know I am a stranger to your universe. I have explained how we came to be here. We were fired on as we passed the city and the ship you sent out was to determine our condition.'

'Of course.' Dobie remained unflustered. 'The chiros?'

'They have their uses. My expedition was into the unknown and I had to take all precautions. If nothing else they served as targets for the . . . the . . . '

'The Groken. The thing which lurks between dimensions and kills,' explained Dobie. 'We call it that. Now we are protected from it but in earlier times — ' Her shrug was expressive. 'So you broke through and immediately attacked our ships. Three destroyed without warning.' Steel edged her voice. 'Do you expect us to thank you for that?'

'It was an accident.' Edallia repeated her previous explanation. 'We were confused, disorientated, firing at random and hoping to throw off the Groken. It probed our hydee and then we were suddenly over Gorm. You fired on us. We crashed.' Edallia spread her hands in a gesture signifying termination. 'That's all.'

'Not quite.' The Lady Dobie was precise. 'You were heading from the wreck in column when found.'

'There was no point in staying. I loaded the chiros and ordered my companions to carry what they could. Water, food, other things such as — '

'Guns!' The interrogator was sharp. 'You carried arms.'

'Of course.'

'You miss my point. Your chiros were carrying them.'

'Why not?' Edallia remained bland. 'What else are such things for but to serve?' She frowned then smiled as if with sudden amusement. 'I see. You think they shouldn't have been trusted with them. How foolish — what chiro would dare to rebel against its mistress?'

A good question and one carrying

interesting implications but they were not to be gone into now. As other questions could wait — all would be answered in time.

Venicia Dobie rose from her chair, smiling, extending a hand in greeting.

'Edallia Kramer you are welcome among us. There is still much to discuss but that can wait until another time. Now you would be more interested in food, wine, a warm bath and a soft bed. Yes?'

'Of course, but I'd be more interested still in getting command of another ship.'

'Later, perhaps. We will talk about the possibility.' Dobie touched a button and to the girl who answered the summons said, 'Arlien, this is Captain Edallia Kramer. Please escort her to her quarters. Attend her.'

Arlien was young, barely a woman, but she had the same blonde hair and blue eyes, the same aggressive femininity as Lamprect and the other women of her crew. Edallia followed her down passages and up winding flights of stairs to a door that opened to reveal comfortable rooms. The girl explained their function as she moved from one to the other.

'The bedroom, my lady. The living room and there is the bathroom. Shall I prepare a bath for you? You'll need clothing — you'll find it in the cabinets. Some wine?' She lifted a decanter. 'No? Food then?' A tray bore a dish of assorted viands. Another, smaller, held what seemed to be decorated chocolates. 'If you wish I can order you something from the kitchen.'

'No.'

'I can prepare your bath and the meal will be here before you have finished taking it.'

'Stop fussing, girl.' Edallia stretched, now more aware of the ache in bruised muscles, the tension numbing her bones. 'Pour me some wine and prepare a bath. Make it hot.'

The wine was darkly emerald served in a goblet of decorated crystal and Edallia held it as she moved to the window. The drapes had yet to be drawn and the city beyond the panes was drenched in a peculiar umber glow. One like a misty fog or moonlight drifting through a gentle haze. In it she could see small glimmerings as if of distant stars. The sun had long since vanished; a scatter of brilliant lights lit the city marking junctions and major roads. From where she stood she could see no sign of a landing field.

'Your bath, my lady.' Arlien was beside her. 'Let me help you to disrobe.'

The water was as ordered and Edallia relaxed in its steaming embrace. Bruises showed on three places on her body and the girl pursed her lips at the sight and added liquids to the water. They stung a little then brought a healing calm.

'You are tense, my lady.' Arlien was on her knees beside the bath, her hands immersed in the water, her fingers busy at their work. A massage that teased the strain from tendon and muscle, and created a flood of mounting comfort. 'Relax, my lady. Close your eyes. Drift, my lady. Let me comfort you.' Her hands moved, moved again. 'Just float on a tide.'

One that held pleasant associations; warmth, sunlight, softness, assurance, the hint of comforting smells, the stir of wakened emotions.

Drifting, Edallia relived the stimulation of battle, the heady euphoria of danger, the relief found in satiated desire. The fingers massaging her became hands that caressed, roving her body with an enticing balm, soothing, luring, guiding, stimulating.

'More wine, my lady?' The hands withdrew as Edallia sat upright in the bath. 'Or shall I finish the massage with oil?'

'Later.' Edallia rose. 'Dry me.'

The towel was warm and as soft as a cloud. The hot air which followed drove away the last of the moisture then the girl was back, hands filled with cream, an unguent she rubbed well into the skin and which vanished as she worked.

Edallia said, dryly, 'Do all who come to the city get this treatment?'

'Not all, my lady. You are special.'

'Because I'm a stranger?'

'You commanded a ship. I would like to ride on a ship.' Arlien paused in her ministrations. 'Would you take me with you? Make me one of your crew?'

'Perhaps. When you're old enough.'

'I'm old enough now. I know my duties.

I would be of great help. Please, my lady? Please say you will.' The lashes lowered over the vivid blue eyes, lifted again. 'I'll do anything you want, my lady. Anything at all if you'll take me.'

Kill? Steal a ship? Betray her people? Edallia doubted it and there was nothing else the girl could give she wanted.

'I'll think about it.'

'You promise?'

'I promise.' Edallia yawned. 'I'm tired. Where's that bed?'

Sitting on it, dressed in a gown of transparent fabric, she reached for the tray and chose a wedge of brownish substance dusted with white flecks. It tasted of meat blended with nuts and spices all of unfamiliar flavours. She ate another then reached for the smaller dish with the chocolate delicacies. As she lifted one she caught sight of Arlien staring at her.

'Something wrong?' Edallia bit into the chocolate and grabbed for the wine. The taste was as if her mouth had been filled with a stinging slime. 'What the hell's this?'

'For the chiros, my lady.' Arlien

sounded her disappointment. 'For when they attend you. During the night,' she explained as Edallia stared at her. 'Or at any other time you might choose to use their services. Do you want me to provide a selection?'

'No.' Edallia took a mouthful of wine, rinsed her mouth, spat it back into the goblet. 'Damned aphrodisiac. Get rid of it. Those too.' She waved at the tray. 'Then leave me to sleep.'

'Alone, my lady?'

'Yes, my dear. Alone.'

To lie on the soft, wide bed and look at the ceiling illuminated with reflections from the window. To see faces in those reflections as if they were a kaleidoscope of ever-changing patterns. Eunice and Daphne, Anne and Natalie. Sylvia Kiouza who made up the last of those women who had survived the battle and wreck. Were they getting special treatment?

Edallia doubted it — only she had claimed to be the captain and only she matched the women of this place in hair and eye colour. In height and build. The product of specialised breeding, she guessed, and wondered if they were alone. Surely others must have broken through limbo and escaped the ravages of that thing — the Groken. The Groken, an amusing nane, she wondered who had invented it.

Who had invented the chocolates, too — an essential ingredient in any society using men as sexual playthings.

She wondered why they hadn't thought of the Harden pump. If anywhere here it would be welcome. Maybe she would teach them about it. Sell the technique, maybe. Set herself up in business as a dealer and provider of chiros all with guaranteed performance.

The thought amused her and she laughed, the patterns on the ceiling swirling in a riot of confusion so that, too late, she thought of the wine and the drugs it could have contained, then fatigue claimed her and she sank into a warm, soft, endless pit of encompassing darkness, still looking at the ceiling, seeing the fading pattern of images but totally unaware of the watchful eye of a scanning lens.

18

Venicia Dobie had always liked the night. It was a time made for intrigue when natural defences were at their weakest and biological fatigue dulled the sharp edge of opposing wills. She had used it as she had used much else in her climb to power. Now, for the first time in years, she sensed just how precarious her position was.

A stranger, arriving from nowhere — was she what she claimed to be?

Dobie looked at the sleeping figure depicted in the screen. One that moved a little, short blonde hair framing a resolute face, lips which must have known the taste of passion. A body that had revealed hard-living despite its feminine beauty. One a little different to the ideal but close enough to allow of argument. Was she of the Scandhar? Could she be?

To the other woman in the room she said, 'Well?'

'She's clever.'

'And?'

Liza Olenya took her time in answering. Younger than her questioner she wore her hair long in thick braids which hung over her shoulders and, when loosed, formed a curtain for her breasts. Now her torso was covered by a thin armour of glittering scales, her hips with a kittle of decorated leather banded with ornate designs. Her legs and arms were nude. Her boots winked with the gleam of gold as did the hilt of the dagger at her belt, the pommel of her whip.

An ambitious woman. One who yearned to rule but had still to learn to master her passions. In a decade she could become a dangerous opponent but, for now, she was an ally.

She said, slowly, 'Her story has holes. The basic facts could well be true; we know ships break through and run the risk of being attacked by the Groken. If they were firing at the time it would account for the unprovoked attack. And yet — ' She broke off, musing, staring at the figure in the screen. 'Has the wreck been thoroughly examined?'

'Yes.' Dobie touched the report. 'Lamprect was a fool,' she said dispassionately. 'She moved too fast. She should have waited and watched before landing — well, it's done now. As to the wreck it is just what we would expect a vessel from beyond to be. Stranger than most and far better armed but still without any form of defensive screen. The thing that worries me is that Edallia is the only member of the crew to resemble the Scandhar. If there were others they had died and been disposed of before landing, but I doubt if any existed. And the chiros. So many chiros!'

'Twenty of them.' Olenya flared her nostrils. 'All prime specimens. A fortune!'

'Which is why Edallia needs to be treated with special consideration. If she can afford to carry so many — and others must have died, did die, their bodies were found, we need to know her source of supply.'

'And once we have that — ' Olenya's whip lashed against her boot. 'Disposition?'

'The dead in the Vazela. The other women

have been housed. Two could have associations with the Romesh but all can be utilised as host-mothers. The ship must be inspected again and stripped of everything of value. Perhaps it should be destroyed, there is no Vazela aboard and, as far as can be determined, no accommodation for one.'

'And the chiros?'

'Sold. What else?'

'Sold,' agreed Olenya. The whip cracked again as she sent the lash against her boot. 'But not too quickly. And not to just the highest bidder. I have the feeling that something could be learned from them.' The whip slashed again at the leather enclosing her foot and calf. 'I know just how to do it.'

A woman who would relish the task and Dobie remembered things whispered about her. Items she recalled after the woman had gone; chiros whipped to pulpy ruin, others driven mad, some used for outrageous experiments. A sadistic drive that fretted her patience and sent her into screaming rages during which none were safe.

The screen flickered as she switched on the mechanism, blurred as she selected a particular scanner. One that showed the initial housing pen and the bodies it contained. Chiros now cleaned, collared, ready for inspection. The kilts they wore barely covered their loins, sandals were scraps of leather to protect their feet. Prime specimens as Olenya had said, unharmed aside from minor injuries.

Which would she buy?

That one with the drawn face and broken arm now cradled in a sling? The young one with golden hair and the features of an ancient god? The dark one who scowled? The lithe one who seemed asleep? The hard one with the face of a pagan idol? Him? That one? Him?

A game and Venicia Dotiie indulged herself knowing that Liza had already made up her mind. It would be a test of her own intelligence to follow the other's line of reasoning and, for a moment, she savoured the pleasure of anticipating her choice and making the purchase herself. A temptation discarded as soon as considered; this was no time to make enemies.

From where he sat Varl watched the movement of the scanner. Not obviously; the last thing he wanted was to attract attention, but if he was to escape this trap he must learn everything available about this new world. So he shifted a little as if to ease his muscles, slumping again in apparent sleep, his eyes mere slits as he gleaned every detail.

They were few enough. The place in which he and the others had been put was just a three-sided shed, roofed with tiles, floored with stone, the open side a grill of thick, iron bars containing a single door, also of bars. A prison cell or a cattle pen; it could have been either as it would have served to hold wild beasts.

Beyond the grilled barrier lay an open area containing a block sided with steps. Ringing it a wall was topped with vicious metal spikes. Against the umber glow of the sky the roofs of buildings showed in a variety of shapes; peaked, spired, domed, some castellated, others more like towers than dwellings.

Varl stirred again, looking at the scanner, one openly flaunted but now still. Whoever had been watching had satisfied their curiosity or had switched the mechanism to a wide-scan node.

From his place down the compound Chatto rose, yawned, stretched, himself and padded over to an open drain where he urinated. Water had been provided and he drank, rinsing his mouth, squaring his shoulders as he looked around. Light caught the swarthy complexion of his face, the thick hair sprouting on limbs and chest. Casually he wandered back to slump down beside Varl.

'No guards,' he whispered. 'At least none that I could see. They must figure we're safe enough in here.'

From where he sprawled to the other side of Varl Zuber said, 'How about the roof? Couldn't we break out there?'

'Sure — and go where?' Varl sat upright, tired of pretence. It was natural they should talk and he guessed there would be nothing now to learn until dawn. 'There could be electronic alarms. If we try escaping and are caught they'll be more wary. Even if we got away from here they'd catch us in the streets. We just

234

don't know enough yet to make the attempt.'

'Cattle.' Chatto spat. 'Those bitches treat us like cattle.'

From the very first when they had been loaded on the alien ship, stripped of weapons and loads, separated from the women and locked in a dark hold. Then to the compound to be stripped, washed down with stinging hoses, collared, kilted, given a bowl of stew and bread. Rich food; there was no point in starving valuable property. The men who had attended them, collared and kilted also, had said nothing.

'Kendrick said this is just what happened to him.' Zuber looked to where the man lay genuinely asleep. 'He reckons that we'll be inspected tomorrow then put up for sale. We could be separated. If we hope to make a plan we'd better think of something now.'

'Seduce the bitches, make them fall for us, then turn against them.' Chatto spat again to signify his contempt. 'Wring their damned necks. How the hell did so many of them get here, anyway?'

'Natural increase,' said Zuber.'

'How? A single ship, maybe, say a couple of hundred crazy women wanting to set up a culture of their own. Breaking through limbo into this universe. Landing on this world. Then what? They'd have to build — hell, from what I've seen and what Kendrick says there must be millions of them.'

'Billions.'

'From one ship?'

'Natural increase,' said Zuber again. 'Say they arrived two hundred years ago. If fifty of them had a child each year for twenty years there would have been a thousand more at the end of that time. Say half of those had done the same. Then half again and so on. In a century you'd have ten million. In two — ' He shrugged. 'Add another five zeros.'

A thousand billion — enough to populate a host of worlds. It wouldn't have been just like that, of course, but near enough and, with labour directed, cities and factories would have sprouted like grain after a summer's rain.

'The women are dominant,' said Zuber.

'We know that. The men must have been used as workers from the beginning. Breeding control would have cut their numbers but they would still have been needed.'

Bred as serfs, conditioned to obey, useful while they were an economic necessity. Varl remembered what he had told Edallia about the basic need that gave birth to slavery. Here it could have been tainted with something else; the detestation of the original settlers for the males of their own species. Feminism run wild. Women hating the very thing they needed; men to work, build, sow, reap, protect, provide while they bore the new generations, Resenting their dependence, shedding it as soon as they could. Then the whip and collar came into its own. The naked domination and, if it hadn't been there all along, the sexual gratification yielded by the demeaning of masculine pride.

'They look alike,' said Chatto. 'I watched them as we were loaded into the ship. Tall, blonde, well-stacked. They could have been sisters.'

'They probably are,' said Zuber. 'Biologically speaking. Parthenogenesis,' he explained. 'Take an egg from a selected woman, fertilise it by artificial stimulus, replant it in her womb and you get an identical copy of the mother. And it needn't be her womb. Her egg could be implanted into any other woman of child-bearing capacity and the result would be the same. They must have aimed for a special strain,' he mused. 'One of the early boss-women, perhaps. Or an ideal containing attributes they all shared. The Scandhar. Kendrick told me they call themselves the Scandhar. Mean anything?'

'Scandinavia,' said Varl. 'A northern region of Earth.' He added, 'I did some checking when I read the report. The women there were emancipated long before the Debacle. There were legends about warrior-women. Not Amazons, something else.' He couldn't remember the name. 'Being so close to the pole they needed plenty of ultraviolet so blondes had a natural advantage.'

'They can go as crazy as anyone else.'

Chatto ran a hand over his own dark thatch. 'Madden's signalling. I guess he wants you.'

The doctor looked up from where he sat beside the man with the broken arm. He grunted as Varl squatted beside him.

'Complications,' he said. 'Teleman's in a bad way.'

The man looked as if he were dying. He sat with his back leaning against the wall, the sling cradling his broken arm dark with sweat. More glistened on his face, his naked torso. Pain had deepened the lines running from nose to mouth making him look older than he was.

'Internal injuries,' said the doctor. 'And maybe some kind of infection. I doped him after the crash but the drugs are wearing off.' He touched the man's forehead, let his fingers linger on the throat. 'Heart's erratic and temperature's way up.'

'What can you do?'

'Here? Nothing.' Madden was emphatic. 'We've no drugs, no facilities, no instruments.'

'How long?'

'Until he dies?' Madden shrugged. 'A

day, maybe two. If his spleen is damaged too badly he's not going to get over it without surgery.' He said, sharply, as Varl reached for Teleman's throat. 'No! Not that!'

'You didn't argue back at the ship.'

'Because there was no point. Those others were beyond help and you did what had to be done. This is different. Those women can't be savages. When they come for us you must demand they help.'

'Me?'

'Who else? You're the Commander.'

And so responsible for them all. Varl rose and stepped to the bars. The sky seemed lighter than before and he guessed it was nearing dawn. Had they escaped they could have found the field by now. Have stolen a ship and be well on their way. The women would have had to be abandoned, of course, but at least they would never be slaves. They could even have been rescued at a later date.

Had they escaped.

If they hadn't been stopped, shot down, left lying in the streets. Taken prisoner and flogged to pulped ruin as an example to others. Turned into things of horror to hop and shamble about the city to provide debased entertainment to titivate the amusement of degenerate women.

A gamble with the odds against them stacked too high for Varl to take.

'Kurt?' Koslenko was at his side. 'I've been checking the scanner. It's crude but effective enough. I could jam it or ruin its function if you want.'

'What will that get us?'

'If anyone is monitoring this place they'll send in a repair crew. When they come we could take over.' Koslenko's hands closed as if on a throat. 'Take their place and open up a way out of here.'

Varl said, 'Teleman's bad. Madden says he's dying.'

'So?'

'If we break out he has to stay. Are you willing to leave him behind?'

Chatto would have had no doubt. Burchard now lost in sleep. Hunter, Quinten, Aynard — the majority of those in the compound. Men with no time for sentimental weakness. If you were starving you ate your dead. If a man was too badly hurt to keep up he was left behind with a gun or given a merciful end. What you needed you took. When you fought you fought to kill.

As Koslenko hesitated Varl said, 'It doesn't matter. We need to know more than we do before we can try anything.'

Koslenko nodded, gripping the bars as he stared at the sky. He had demonstrated a weakness and wondered how long it would be before he had grown as cynical as Varl and the wolves he had brought from Hell. Or maybe it was that they had accepted a reality he had never known. Always he had known law and order; the protection of others given in return for his obedience. Now he had to rely on himself.

'It's a long night,' he said. 'If it was winter it would be colder than it is.'

'On Earth,' agreed Varl. 'This isn't Earth.'

'No.' Koslenko looked at his hands, the grip he had taken on the bars. Small muscles quivered in his forearms. 'Have we any hope?'

Varl was confident. 'We'll get out of this. The women are free and they won't forget us. All we need do is watch and wait and act when the time is right.'

'And while we wait we bow and scrape and be the toys of a bunch of vicious bitches.' Koslenko released his grip on the bars. The metal had left deep imprints on his fingers and palms. 'We could end up like Kendrick did. Scarred, beaten, broken, cringing — God!'

'It can happen.' Varl turned to look at the others. Kendrick had kept himself apart and now lay curled as if in sleep. 'But only if you let it. Look on it as a game,' he urged. 'Act the part, pretend, pit your cunning and intelligence against theirs. It shouldn't be hard. Just let them think you are what they want you to be. Watch and wait and learn then, when the moment comes — ' His hand made a chopping gesture.

Good advice; Koslenko wondered if he could take it.

19

Dawn came with a tintinnabulation of bells; a musical chiming which rose from every roof and upper wall as the wind hit metal and glass to create a medley of sound.

Edallia heard it and was at once awake, rearing up on the bed, wide-eyed, relaxing as she determined the cause, sinking back into the soft, warm embrace.

Liza Olenya ignored it; it was a sound she had heard most of her life, one as familiar as her heart beat. Beside the bed the chiro turned on his mat, aware of her interest, opening his eyes to meet her hostile glare.

'My lady.' He was up and facing her, body bent, head lowered, arms spread in obeisance. 'What is your desire?'

More ships, more crews, the position now held by Venicia Dobie. More wealth and more power and the answers to questions that had gnawed her during the night. Ones the fool standing before her couldn't even imagine much less answer.

'Prepare my bath,' she snapped. 'But before that — you did not please me last night.'

He cringed as she rose and reached for her whip.

'My lady — I beg you!'

To lace him with welts would be easy; to cut open the flesh merely a matter of extra effort. Had he backed she would have done it; the punishment merited by his disobedience. No slave should try to avoid the whip. As it was she sent the lash to sting his buttocks, hitting him again as she felt the remembered pleasure. Again as she sensed her power. Only when he collapsed at her feet, whining, did she throw aside the whip.

'My bath. Hurry.'

After he would be returned to the pool to mingle with the rest of the chiros selected for their entertainment value. She must remember not to use him again. Deference, at certain times, lacked a desired stimulus and yet what else could a chiro provide? Even the best of them were limited to a mechanical rhythmic ability, some well-taught manipulative techniques, words which held emptiness because mouthed by rote. Novelty could titivate a little but never was there true spontaneity. Always she felt dissatisfied.

Now blood was the answer. Not from the resident stock but that provided by those found in the Spiral. The reason for their inflated value; being unconditioned each provided a unique challenge. And, if somewhere was an unlimited supply — trust Venecia think of the obvious.

Bathed, dressed, Olenya headed for the tower-like building which housed the Principal and her guest. Venicia herself, having retired late, was still asleep but had left no interdict against Edallia receiving callers. She turned as Olenya entered the room, eyes narrowing as if she feared attack, widening as the other introduced herself.

'Marshal Olenya? That means — '

'I control half the ships of Gorm.' Liza dismissed the fact as of small consequence. 'Did you sleep well?'

Edallia nodded. 'Half the ships, you

246

say? Then Venicia Dobie — '

'Controls the other half and has senior command. That makes her the Principal of Gorm. Was the chiro to your liking?' As Edallia made no reply Olenya continued, 'If not I could, perhaps, be of help. My own household contains several you might find of interest. Better yet you could make your own purchases.' She clapped her hands as if the idea had suddenly occurred to her. 'As a captain you have certain privileges as to prior choice.'

'But no credit,' said Edallia dryly. She wondered at the other's motive; such a woman would have no need and less desire to cultivate friends. 'Unless my ship can be sold as scrap.'

'Not your ship, my dear, your chiros. Have you forgotten? Come, first we'll have breakfast then we'll visit the compound. Do you like seethed grantle? Boiled raskaoh eggs? Fried loraas? I know a place which serves them all.'

One that rested on a boulevard leading from the wide plaza occupying the heart of the city. Hylda showed its beginnings in a dozen ways; old houses carefully protected against the ravages of time, others newer but blending into the general pattern. One of cautious development and wary expansion. The plaza and boulevards were of more recent origin but the path they had taken to reach it had wended through narrow alleys and bleak-walled dwellings. Concrete history protected against wanton despoiling; with worlds to play with why rip down in order to rebuild?

Edallia relaxed in her chair as a waiter served the initial tisane. Hylda was one of a dozen large cities on Gorm and in it, as the others, the day commenced at dawn. Already the streets were thronged with traffic and pedestrians, the ships open, the air humming with normal activity. Chiros swept the sidewalks and gutters, others ran on mysterious errands, some, like the waiter, worked in shops and service-departments. All were collared, but some were a little more than decoration. All were obsequious,

'My lady.' The waiter was at her side, a tray balanced on his left hand, serving tongs poised in his right. 'Some grantle?

A few raskach eggs? Or would you care to try the scrarnbled olmate?'

Edallia said, 'Feed me something solid. I leave the choice to you.'

Olenya was more particular choosing eggs, lomas, a portion of something that looked like brawn and several spoonfuls of a granulated powder. For some time she concentrated on the food then, dabbing her lips with a napkin, leaned back in her chair.

'Berthe certainly knows how to manage her cooks,' she said. 'Buying this place was the best investment she ever made.'

'You know her?'

'One of my captains. Too old now, of course, but she served well and I'm pleased to see she is making a go of things.' Olenya sipped at her tisane. 'I always think that a person needs to consider her future. Some-times she can use a little help and advice. Especially when she is a stranger.'

'As I am?' Edallia smiled. 'Before I forget I must thank you for the tour of the city and the explanations. You have been most kind.'

Olenya reached for her tisane. 'We are

both ship-captains and have much in common. I understand that you are eager to gain a new command. I might be able to help you. The final decision rests with the Principal of course but, well, something could be arranged.'

At a price, naturally, and Edallia wondered just what it would be. She took a sip of her tisane, savouring the warm, herb-scented liquid, feeling more relaxed now that Olenya had come out into the open. Greed, ambition, bribery, opportunism were things she could understand and deal with. More ard more of this universe showed comfortable similarities to her own.

'I said you were kind.' Edallia's smile reached her eyes. 'If you could help me I'd be most grateful. I'm that already, of course, but a woman needs to know where she stands and I would really like a command. Once you've known space, well — you don't need telling, Marshal.'

'Liza.' Olenya lifted a hand to signal for the bill. 'Call me Liza. Friends have no need for formality.'

'Not off-duty,' agreed Edallia. It was as

well to register the fact that she would not be too pushing. 'The next time we eat together you must let me pay.'

Outside the sun had warmed the air, filling it with the scent of flowers, with tinkles as vagrant breezes stirred the rooftop bells. Around them the pedestrians seemed all of a kind then, as Edallia studied them, small differences became obvious. Height was often achieved by extra-high heels, hair given added brightness by tints and dyes. Eyes were not always the same vivid blue, and figures were enhanced by artifice. The Scandhar were not all perfect but all strove to emulate the common ideal.

Those closest to it held the highest positions; the inevitable result of selective breeding and a system in which the elite chose who would be the elite. Others did all the things that required intelligence and responsibility,

Slaves did the rest.

Edallia looked at a group of them busy tending the flowers that grew in beds linking the boulevard. They worked with a grim, mechanical attention to the task. An attitude probably induced by their over-seer who lounged with a whip in her hand on a bench close by.

'You like them?' Olenya had noticed her interest. 'Don't waste time on such rubbish. They can offer you nothing. A year or two and — ' Her whip cut the air. 'You know what happens then.'

An assumption but Edallia nodded. A slave-owner should know what happened to discarded slaves. As a captain should know how to operate a vessel — and she was no captain. She wondered if Olenya would require a test of her proficiency and if she could bluff her way to acceptance. The ship would be different so there would have to be tuition as regards the controls. This universe was different so it would be natural for her to lack knowledge as to its structure. The engines? They could be different too. Given the chance she could manage and there would have to be a trained crew. Basically a captain needed only give commands.

They reached the end of the boulevard and entered the wide plaza. A fountain adorned the centre, one ringed with flowers, water falling to drench attendant statues. All were depictions of women, tall, heroic, heads thrown back to stare at the sky, the freedom it offered. The symbolism was unmistakable.

'The First,' explained Olenya. 'They settled Gorm and made the pact with the Vazela. While time lasts they will be honoured.'

'The Vazela?'

'Others.' Olenya made no attempt to explain. 'We must come back here later. At night when the statues are illuminated there is an atmosphere here then. Almost you can hear them speaking.'

The water would do that. The murmur as it rushed over the stone coupled with the rustle of leaves, the sigh of gentle winds. Edallia glanced at her companion as she led the way across the plaza. Not superstitious. On that she would bet, so why the visit to the statues? The dedication? And who were the Vazela?

Shops fronted the far end of the plaza many filled with bright clothing, leather-work, metal plates hammered into various shapes. As they passed one a girl ran from the interior.

'Marshal! Marshal Olenya!'

'Tana!' Olenya came to a halt. 'How nice to see you.'

The girl was like Arlien, young, tall, her face bright with pleasure. She lifted both hands in greeting as she neared Olenya to touch her, embracing her as their cheeks met. The whip dangling from her wrist was new.

Olenya glanced at it as they parted.

'Why, Tana, you own a chiro!'

'Only a fifth,' she confessed. 'The others on my floor agreed to share. We didn't get much but it's good enough to do the cleaning and,' she lifted her wrist to display the whip, 'it gives us status.'

'Of course. Isn't it wonderful, Edallia?'

'Is it?'

'Tana wants to enter the training academy but getting accepted isn't easy. Too few ships, you understand. Even if we had twice as many we could fill them. Everyone wants to get into space. So I advised her to get a chiro. It helps to establish your position.'

Edallia said, spitefully, 'Even a part of one?'

'It still makes you an owner. Like crews, they carry whips even though, technically, they only have part use of a ship's chiro. I assume your customs are different.' Olenya's eyes drifted to the bareness of Edallia's wrists. 'But then I expect — '

A scream interrupted her. A hoarse, animal-like sound that came from the interior of a shop lower down. Other sounds followed it, different, the shrieking of a woman, the cries of others in hysterical rage.

'Hold it!'

'Stop the chiro!'

'Beat it down!'

A man came running from the shop. He was stooped, wild-eyed, hands extended before him, fingers curved into claws. Blood dropped from his shoulders, smeared the fabric of his kilt. The corners of his mouth held foam.

'There!' The woman chasing him was tall, broad, face twisted in anger. The whip in her hand lifted, pointed. 'Rape!' she screamed. 'Rape!'

'No!' The man lifted his hands in

255

appeal. 'I didn't do it. No!'

A lash tore open his cheek. Another cut stained his side with a carmine smear. A third and he was running, hands beating the air before him, heading directly to where Edallia was standing,

'Get him!' Olenya was sharp. 'Cut him down — '

Without a whip that wasn't possible but there were other ways to stop him and they would be more merciful. Edallia swayed as he neared her, moved to thrust her leg between his own, blocked a wildly swinging fist and, with a quick movement, had him sprawled on the ground.

'Good.' Olenya shoved her aside. 'Who accuses this chiro?'

'I do.' The woman clutched a torn dress to her bosom. 'He just came at me. Tried to force me. I clawed at his shoulder as he pushed me down.' She pointed to the scratches. 'See?'

'Your punishment?'

'Death!' The one who had first used the whip yelled the answer. 'Rapist! Kill the animal!'

'You weren't asked. You — ' Olenya

broke off as the man heaved, breaking the grip of those who held him. 'Stand clear!'

She struck as he climbed to his feet, sending the lash across his eyes. A calculated blow that ruined his sight and left him, hands lifted to his face, screaming as whips lashed at his body. Olenya's joined by others; women pushing forward to strike in turn, struggling for the opportunity. Tana was among the first.

Edallia stepped well back, masking her face as she watched. The entire thing had been a setup, of that she was certain. The early talk, the hint of advancement, the girl with the whip, even the detour to linger at the statues so as to kill time. Then the poor devil used as bait. He must have been drugged. Edallia remembered the foam on his lips. A man terrified of what was to come. In any woman-dominated society rape was a serious charge. Add the love of using the whip and the end was a foregone conclusion.

An expensive way to discover — what? Edallia looked at her bare wrists. No whip — and on Gorm to own a slave was to carry a whip. Did the Marshal suspect her of lying? If so she was in trouble, alone, without funds, on a hostile world. Had she been tested? Was the whole thing merely an effort to bolster the price of later favours?

'Marshal!' Edallia called out as the man sank moaning to the ground, 'Liza!'

'What is it?' Olenya turned, breathing deeply, her tone impatient. Flecks of blood dappled her face and clothing. The whip she held was a carmine strand dripping blood. 'What do you want? Quick! He's going!'

'That's why I called you.' Edallia showed her bare wrists. 'Can you lend me the price of a whip?'

20

With the bells had come food; more stew served in wooden bowls eaten with a spoon of similar material. As the day brightened early visitors had passed through the spiked wall to stand and stare and pass lewd and rude comments, women who had bribed the attendants and guards for a special viewing.

'You!' One pointed at Zuber. 'Come closer, Turn. Give me your head.' She ran her fingers through his golden mane. 'Now strip.'

Zuber hesitated, looking at Varl, reading the message in his eyes. Reluctantly he obeyed.

'Come closer. That's better.' The woman prodded, gripped, squeezed. 'A fine body. How virile are you? What have you been taught? How many can you serve in a night?'

'With respect, my lady, I am not your chiro. For answers you must ask my owner.'

'You dare to defy me!'

'My lady we are the property of Captain Edallia Kramer.' Varl was quick to the rescue. 'Damage us and she will hold you responsible.' He added, as if eager to please, 'The Captain is quick to anger.'

A warning the woman chose to heed. The whip lowered and she turned to stalk from the area. Others followed and, once again, the space beyond the bars was deserted.

'Damned bitch!' Chatto spat through the grill. 'Handling a man as though he was a dog. What the hell have we got into?'

Trouble and of more than one kind. Madden rose from beside Teleman, a damp rag in his hand. It had done nothing to break the fever. As Varl watched he marched to the door set into the wall and began to pound on it with a fist. He might as well have pounded the wall.

'Take it easy.' Varl gripped his wrist, saved his hand from further damage. 'What's wrong?'

'Teleman's dying. You know that. It's time we got some kind of help.'

'We'll get it. Koslenko!'

The scanner had been moving, now it froze as the officer jammed it, ruining it before dropping from Burchard's shoulders. As he landed he staggered, clutching Varl's arm as he almost fell.

'We should have done this last night.' He was bitter. 'How can we escape during the day?'

'We can't. Hunter! Aynard! All of you! Get into motion.'

A gamble — but all life was a gamble. Varl dropped as did the others, panting, limp, a man obviously far from well. The others followed his example, falling so as to whisper without detection, a pattern that allowed the passing of messages. Soon those doing the monitoring would come to fix the scanner. Last night they would have ignored it but soon the potential buyers would arrive and expect everything to be normal.

'Remember,' whispered Varl. 'We're all ill. Teleman's bad and we caught something from him.'

'Those women know different.' Chatto spoke from where he lay to one side.

'They won't talk. They came early to jump the gun. The guards will keep silent too. Anyway, this thing has just hit us.'

The only weapon they had — the fear of disease that must be present in any society. If nothing else the sale would be delayed and they would send for Edallia. If smart she would demand they be held in quarantine under her control. The other women, also suspect, could be gathered and isolated with them. Then they could plan their escape.

If the women cooperated.

If Edallia chose to help.

A thought that Varl had pondered during the night. She was too much like the Scandhar and, if accepted, might decide to make her own way. It could be a pleasant one once she had sold her property. If she was allowed to retain it. If the masquerade wasn't discovered.

But the last didn't really matter. She had the upper hand. Varl's fear was that she would use it.

'Kendrick said they'd use their whips,'

Quinter said, passing the word. 'What if they do?'

'You take it. We all take it. Damn it, what the hell did we decide on last night?'

'If I get grabbed and handled like Jac I'll — '

'Take it!' Varl mastered his temper. 'Just think yourself lucky. I've known men who've paid for treatment like that. You'd be getting it free. No more talk, now. We're too ill to chat.'

But not too ill to sweat, to suffer the pain of knotting cramps, the tightening of stomachs and the tension which drew nerves into quivering strings. Only Teleman, drifting in a world of delirium, was free of the torment of waiting.

Then, finally, they came.

'Ill?' Edallia stared her disbelief. 'Really ill?'

'So it would seem.'

'All of them?'

The physician nodded. To her there was no doubt; chiros did not lie. Nor did they dare to sabotage equipment. 'The monitoring scanner fell out of order most probably because of a desperate attempt to summon assistance. Naturally none has yet been provided in view of the unusual circumstances.' She added, 'The sale was immediately cancelled.'

Which accounted for the empty area, the deserted block. Even the guards were invisible. Edallia looked for them then at the space beyond the bars. The floor was littered with somnolent figures.

'A pity.' Olenya, at her side, sounded regretful.

'The sale could have been entertaining. You could have turned your assets into a modest fortune. Now, unfortunately, the holding charges will eat into later profits.'

And put her neck harder on the block.

'All right.' Edallia lifted her whip, gesturing at the door set in the bars, 'Open up. Let's find out what's wrong.'

She entered the compound alone; none of the others were eager to risk catching an alien disease. Varl grunted as she prodded him with her whip.

'I'm alone.' She knelt beside him, her voice a whisper. 'Talk. What's going on?'

'Teleman's dying. He needs medical help. Get it. Have the rest of us put in quarantine.' He told her of his plan. 'I've set it up. Now make it work.'

'But — '

'Don't waste time arguing. Just do as I say.'

Orders — and from a man!

She rose and stood looking down at him, her hand closing on the stock of the whip. An unconscious gesture dictated by annoyance but a natural one for what she pretended to be. She passed among the others, prodding, stooping as if to make examinations. Like Varl they stayed motionless, not even speaking. The smell of them made her nostrils wrinkle.

Teleman groaned when she touched him.

'How bad is he?' She spoke to Madden at his side. 'Really, I mean.'

'Unless he gets help he'll be dead in a matter of hours.' The doctor was bleak. 'If you can't get anything else bring drugs to ease his pain.'

Something Varl could do or most of the others; ending Teleman's agony with a relentless pressure on the carotid arteries which would bring first unconsciousness then death. But the doctor was of a gentler breed.

'I'll do what I can.' Edallia touched the sick man again. 'Now tell me what you could have that knocked you out like this. Something not too dangerous — if they get scared they could burn us all.'

She listened, remembering, rising to complete her apparent examination, pausing at last beside Kendrick. His fear was genuine, the smell of it stronger than the odours of sweat and urine. She felt him jerk as she touched him, the small, automatic bunching of muscles beneath the skin as he responded to his terror.

'It'll be all right,' she soothed. 'If all else fails I'll claim you as my ship-boy. You won't be put on the block.'

An easy promise to make, maybe one hard or impossible to keep, but it would give him courage and keep him quiet. A compromise; killing him would be safer but that could wait. As Edallia reached the door leading to the block-area the physician lifted a hand.

'No further.' Her tone was grim. 'You could have been contaminated.'

Olenya said, 'How serious is it?'

'It's more of an inconvenience than anything else. The chiros will be over it within a week. Good food and vitamins will help. Wash them down, give them somewhere to stay and they'll be ready for the block before you know it.' Edallia looked at the Marshal, appeal in her eyes. 'Please, Liza. This isn't serious.'

No disease could be called that. Even a mild viral infection could run wild among people isolated from it and lacking defensive antibodies.

The physician said, 'They must be destroyed.'

'No!' Edallia glared her anger. 'They are my property. And what of the others? Are you going to destroy the women too? And me? What about me?'

A moment in which her life and that of the others hung poised on a razor's edge. If logical the Scandhar had no choice but to destroy them all and she cursed Varl for his plan and the situation she was now in. Olenya came to the rescue.

'Isolation,' she said. 'They can be kept in isolation. The other women too.'

'I protest.' The physician was harsh. 'To be weak now is to invite disaster.'

Opposition that sealed the decision. No mere healer could be allowed to dictate to a Marshal of Gorm.

'You expect me to stay in this filth?' Edallia stepped into the sunlight. 'It stinks in there. At least you could have hosed them down.'

'Please!' The physician backed as she advanced.

'Stay clear of us. I must insist. Guards!'

They appeared on the summit of the spiked wall. A dozen of them, gleaming in metal-scale armour, faces framed in plumed helmets, armed. The barrels of their weapons focussed on Edallia. She halted, looking at them, at Olenya standing well to one side, at the physician and her aides.

'One of my chiros is dying from the result of physical injuries and should be removed and given immediate medical attention. He needs surgery, antibiotics and intensive care.'

'The others?' The physician ignored the needs Edallia had specified. 'What is wrong with them?'

She shrugged. 'I'm a captain, not a doctor, but it looks to me like dengue.' Edallia described the disease as Madden had told her. 'We must have picked it up on Weephrom — our last call. I've had it before and so am immune. Most of the other women too, I imagine. Have any of them complained of pains? Aching muscles? Dizziness? Loss of balance?' She waited then, as the physician remained silent, added, 'No matter. It usually takes a couple of days longer to show up in females.'

'You!' The physician pointed with her whip, first at Varl then at Zuber. 'And you! Pick him up, and carry him to that door.' To Edallia she said, 'The chiro is your property. You have the right to witness the disposal.'

An odd way to talk of giving medical treatment and Edallia felt her stomach tighten as she followed the others to the designated door. It was thick, barred, as yet untouched by cleansing flame. Beyond it ran a narrow passage terminating in another door. The air held a faint acrid smell.

'Take the injured chiro to the far end. Lay him on the floor. Return to stand as you do now.' The physician spoke from a safe distance. 'Commence.'

The door slammed shut behind them as Varl and Zutier carried Teleman down the passage. When they returned Edallia whispered. 'What the hell's going on?'

Varl grunted, narrowing his eyes as he searched the gloom. The passage could merely be a transition-point to avoid close proximity with those in the compound; in such a place deaths could not be uncommon. The far door could lead to a space outside where a vehicle could carry the sick man to hospital. The acrid smell some form of antiseptic.

'What — ' Zuber jumped as a grill suddenly dropped before them. 'Kurt?'

'It shall be as I order.' Olenya was cold. 'Have them stripped, washed, assembled by the block. Sterilise the compound. Move!' As the attendants rushed to obey she looked at Edallia, stepping closer, halting while still well clear. 'I'm sorry, my dear, but you must join them.'

'In isolation? With chiros?'

'Only until the crisis is over. As you are immune you have nothing to fear. Later we shall get together and this unpleasantness can be forgotten. We have much to discuss and I would like to get close to you.' Olenya lifted her whip, extending her arm, the tip of the stock touching gently against Edallia's cheek, her neck, lingering on her breast. A caress unmistakable in its implication. 'Together there is much we could accomplish.'

Edallia returned her smile, her hand lifting, pressing the whip hard against where it rested. 'You are more than kind, Liza. I look forward to the time when I may be able to show my gratitude. What of the injured chiro?'

'The Vazela will take care of it.'

Teleman had been moved with the rest, more dragged than carried to a place beside the block. He leaned against it, mouth open, breath ragged, sweat dewing his face and body. The others stood around him, swaying, some falling to all fours, at few twisting on the ground. It wasn't all acting; cramps and stiffness affected them all.

271

Varl said nothing, looking at the grill that blocked the passage, at the sick man lying beyond it, at the door at the far end now slowly opening.

'God!' Edallia dug her fingers into his arm. 'What is it?'

A thing like a spider, four feet high, six long, edged with legs, fronted by a devil's mask of jaws, curved mandibles, feathery palps, eyes which gleamed as if with an inner fire. It passed through the door and paused, rearing, antennae quivering. A thing that seemed to study the grill, those standing beyond it, before again moving towards where Teleman lay.

It glided like a ghost, limbs weaving, pausing again to raise its head.

'Kurt! For God's sake — '

'Shut up.' Varl eased the clamping fingers from his arm. 'There's nothing we can do.'

Teleman was in delirium, if he could see the thing at all it would merely be a fragment of his nightmare. The grill was too strong to break and the creature was an unknown threat. Even if they smashed their way towards it, killed it, nothing would have been accomplished. But, watching, they could learn.

The first impression had been false — the thing was not a spider. The illusion had been created by the many limbs, the bizarre head, the stance and movement. The body was smaller than it had seemed; enhanced by the fringe of legs. The coating was fur, smooth, gleaming, striated in black and gold. The legs ended in what could have been pads tipped with claws like those of a crab. The eyes were round, not facetted like those of a fly, but edged with thick ridges and centred with vertical irises like those of a goat. Six of them set around the head and giving, Varl guessed, double the field of vision possessed by a man.

The Vazela.

As they watched it began to feed.

21

In the compound they'd had air, space beyond the bars, a chance to see the sky. Now they were in a long, narrow room, a dozen feet wide, a score high. Sacks littered the floor together with pitchers of water and buckets to take care of natural functions. A single door broke the expanse of the flanking walls. A single window, set high, cast diffused light from one end. It was narrow, barred, unglazed; an opening punched in what had once been a fortress.

Through it Varl looked at the distant field.

It lay at the edge of the city, a broad expanse faced with what had to be repair sheds, warehouses, barracks, workshops, dwellings. On it ships rested like a scatter of toys their hulls burning golden in the fading light of day. A few guards patrolled the area, slow, indifferent. Other figures, chiros, policed the field, collecting rubbish that they placed in sacks slung over their backs.

'Any luck?'

Burchard called from where he stood bearing the weight of Varl's left foot. Beneath him other men formed the human pyramid that Varl had climbed to the window.

'Some. I can see the field. Now let's see if we can get out of here.'

Varl turned his attention to the bars. The door was solid, firmly bolted, the window their only chance of escape. The bars ran vertically, too close to permit of passage between. He gripped them in turn, muscles bunching as he twisted, trying to loosen one in its socket. None yielded. He moved, gripping the longest with both hands, throwing up his legs so as to plant his feet against the edge of the window. An awkward position; the thrust of his knees pushed him away from the bars and ruined his precarious balance. He grunted, adjusted his grip, swore as again he failed to gain leverage.

'Kurt?'

'I'm trying to force apart these bars but

I can't get into position. Send men up here to hold me.'

Burchard was one of them, riding his living support as he supplied a platform with his back and shoulders. Varl lay on it as if on a bed, moving to the end of the window, thrusting his arms between the bars and down to grip one close to the centre. Again he rammed his feet against the stone, gripped harder, fed power to his back and shoulders as he heaved.

It was like pulling at a mountain.

'Send up a sack.'

The metal had cut into his hands. Varl took the sack and wrapped it around the bar. He adjusted his position, thrusting his arms through a different opening, placing his feet with more care. Gripping the bar he waited, breathing deeply, hyperventilating his lungs. Then, with a convulsive effort, he threw all his energy into an explosive effort.

He felt the blood roar in his ears, a hammer begin to strike at his temples, dark patches fogging his vision and then, without warning, the bar bent and tore free.

'Here.' Madden was at his side as others lowered him to the floor. 'Drink and take these.'

The cup held water, the pills were green.

'Salt and vitamins,' said the doctor. 'All Edallia could persuade them to give us.'

'She should have slipped us a knife.' Koslenko, joining them, was bitter. 'Or some clothes — do we have to be naked?' He touched the collar that was his only adornment. 'They treat us like dogs while she rests in luxury. It's easy to guess why. Did you see how that bitch made up to her? A proposition if I ever saw one. No matter what happens to us Edallia will make out.'

Varl said, 'So far she's played along.'

'Sure, so far — but for how much longer? When the chips are down which way will she jump?'

'Our way.' Varl sounded more confident than he felt. He added, 'Get up to the window. Find out what you can. If there are alarms or trip-wires we have to know. Take your time and do a good job but don't let yourself be seen.' As the other hesitated he snapped, 'We have to be ready by dark, man. Move!'

'He's worried,' commented Madden as Koslenko moved away. 'Afraid of what could happen.'

He wasn't the only one. Varl leaned back, easing the soreness of his arms, the ache in back and legs. To one side, men were busy fashioning rope; ripping the sacks into strands with teeth and nails, braiding them into a lengthening coil. Chiros, slaves — unless they could escape they would join the other males to rot at the bottom of the pile.

Varl closed his eyes thinking of Edallia and what Koslenko had said. In this society it would be a matter of personal survival for her to cut free. Chiros, males, were scum to be worked, used, abused; sexual playthings whipped, vasectomised aside from a select few who would be milked of desired sperm. Or perhaps not even that. The one certainty was there could be no genuine love between the sexes. Any woman feeling romantic affection for a male would be considered a deviant — how a man felt didn't matter. True love had to be a unisex affair.

Sparta in reverse; then the males were forced to marry by decree in order to impregnate women and breed new warriors. True love was confined to the fighting men. Sparta, ancient Greece — any culture that demarcated the sexes had the same polarity. Here Lesbos was triumphant; women-love, named for an island, had grown to encompass worlds.

'Varl!'

He blinked, aware that he had dozed, glancing at the window now no longer filled with daylight.

'It's late.' Burchard was at his side. 'Koslenko's checked and there are no alarms from what he could see. You want me to come with you?'

'You follow if I don't make it.' Varl rose, stretched, the rest had washed the ache from his body. 'Has the rope been tested? Good. Let's go.'

He climbed to the top of the human pyramid, catching the coil of rope Chatto threw up to him, slipping it over his shoulder before slipping through the bars. Outside a narrow ledge provided a precarious foothold. Varl balanced himself on it, gripping the bars, looking down to where the wall fell in a sheer, unbroken drop to the street below. Above it rose ten feet to the crenellated edge of the roof. Mortar had fretted from between the stones forming the wall and he dug his fingers into the crack, pulling himself upward, toes searching for holds.

The crenellations were wide, deep, edged with bells. One jangled as Varl slipped beneath it and he froze, eyes searching the umber gloom. The roof was flat, flanked on one side with the shafts of ventilators and what could have been the protected head of a stair. He saw nothing dangerous and rose to move carefully along the edge.

The window he had escaped from was matched by two others running on a line to the east. Both were dark. He frowned, studying the layout of the building. The windows faced towards the edge of the city and, in the old days, must have formed part of a defensive screen. The opposite side would have faced an enclosed courtyard. He crossed to it, looked over the edge and saw patches of light glowing from below.

Windows, wider, lower than those of the far side of the building. One of them could open on the room in which the women were housed.

Varl uncoiled the rope, fastened it to a crenellation and, wary of the bells, eased himself over the edge. The first window showed an empty room. The second a chamber containing lounging guards. The third time he was lucky; Sylvia Kiouza stared, wide-eyed, at him through the panes.

'Commander!'

She fell silent as he lifted a warning finger against his lips. The window was unbarred and he dived through it as she opened it wide. As it closed behind him he looked at the chamber, the women it contained.

'Where's Natalie?'

'With Edallia. She had an argument with a guard and got herself bruised a little.' Sylvia thinned her lips. 'Those damned bitches need to be taught a lesson. They treat us like an inferior species.'

But one still entitled to comforts. The chamber was carpeted, fitted with soft furnishings, wine and cakes standing on a table. Varl helped himself to both.

'We're ready to make a break,' he said. 'If you want to stay now's the time to say so.'

'Stay?' Anne shook her head. 'I've heard talk of what they have in mind for us. Surrogate mothers, that's what. Planted with their fertilised eggs and used as brood-mares. That's not for me.'

'Nor me.' Eunice was as emphatic. 'When you go we go with you. Right Daphne? Sylvia?'

They nodded their agreement. Varl said, 'What about Natalie?'

'She's with us.'

'Edallia?' He noted their hesitation. 'Where is she?'

The women had been provided with comfort, Edallia enjoyed luxury. Varl stepped on a carpet that was as soft as a cloud, breathed air heavy with the scent of flowers. The furnishings were to match; the bed covered with a rich cover of brocaded silk, the chairs designed to hold with the comfort of a palm. There was a bathroom, a shower, a hotplate loaded with succulent viands. Wine rested in a container of ice.

'The good life.' Varl stared at Edallia who had risen from the bed. 'I guess you like it.'

'So?'

'We're making a break. If you don't want to join us you'd better let me know.'

'And if I decide to stay?' She stepped towards him, clean, her body adorned with a clinging gown that emphasized her femininity. 'Will you kill me to shut my mouth?'

'No.' Varl met her eyes. 'But I'll have to make sure you don't betray us.'

'Tie me up? Gag me? Have someone stand guard?'

She smiled with genuine amusement. 'Kurt, darling, I didn't know you cared. It would be so much simpler just to kill me. I guess I should be flattered.'

He said, patiently, 'Are you coming with us?'

'Of course.' Edallia glanced at the woman seated in a chair. Natalie, her face blotched with an ugly bruise, the thin, red line of a lash lying across her neck. 'We'll all go with you. When do you leave?'

'Later, when it's nearing dawn.' A good time for desperate enterprises when fatigue would have dulled the senses of the guards and life would be at its lowest ebb. 'You'll have to get to us. Can you manage that?'

'I guess so. We're all in quarantine, remember. The guards want to stay clear. I'll just check on how my property is fairing. So we get to you. Then what?' She shook her head as he explained. 'No. You'll never make it. Try going downstairs and you'll run into a pack of guards.'

'Then we'll drop from the window. Have the girls bring along as much as they can carry in the way of fabric for ropes, clothing, stuff like that. Some food and wine would help too. Have you any weapons? No? How about knives?'

'Only those we eat with.'

'Sharpen them up.' Varl looked at her and added, 'We'll only have the one chance. Muff it and we'll end up like Teleman.'

'You don't have to remind me.' Her shiver was genuine. 'You'll stay here, of course.'

'No. The others will be wondering what's happened,' he explained. 'If I don't return others will try and could get caught.' He reached out, took her hands, squeezed them. 'It's up to you now. I want you to make it.'

'If we can't?'

'We leave anyway.'

Varl headed back to the other room, the window he had entered by. It swung open and he reached for the rope hanging from above and pushed himself into the open air. Climbing he reached the roof, bells jangling as he squirmed over the crenellations. A harshly musical clangour that seemed to fill the universe. As it died he rose to cross the roof, his path taking him close to the dark blotches of the ventilators, the structure at the top of the stairs.

A nest of umber shadow and, as he neared it, something moved.

A thing he had seen before, multi-legged, striated in black and gold, eyes that glowed like cold fire, mandibles which clicked.

Weight that hit him and threw him down, holding him helplessly on his back.

A vazela — one eager to feed.

22

There was an odour to it; a dry, musty scent like that of a cat. One matching the softness of the fur that clothed the body and limbs with a silken down. A covering for flesh and muscle surrounding the rigid bars of bone. Not an insect then; the shape had given that illusion, one augmented by the contours of the head, the row of eyes, the palps, the curved mandibles which closed on his throat like the dagger-jaws of pincers.

Luck saved him. Varl had fallen with his hands lifted to protect his face, his wrists now in line with his throat, trapped within the closing mandibles. As the tips touched his skin he tensed his muscles, pushing out with his wrists, moving the sharp points away from his flesh.

A victory won with tremendous strain; the leverage was against him. One he would soon lose, the weight of the creature resting on his chest constricted his lungs and made breathing a nightmare. Soon he would weaken, his arms lose their power; when they did the poised mandibles would strike home.

The prelude to a nauseating death.

Varl heaved, rearing, arching his back in a desperate effort to break free. Legs scrabbled around him as the thing moved, trapping him in a cage of living tissue, pressing him back to the surface of the roof. Palps quivered, hanging poised, dropping to rest on Varl's face.

A voice echoed in his mind.

'Why do you resist me?'

'What? Can you talk?'

'We can communicate. While I touch you our minds can meet. Why do you resist me?'

'I don't want to die.'

'I do not understand. You were warned not to leave your quarters on pain of death. Leaving them you knew you would die. Therefore you came seeking death. Yet you resist me.'

The cold logic of a machine. For a moment Varl was tempted to lie but the warning had been given and the thing could probably tell if he ventured from the truth.

To defeat it he must attack it on its own ground.

'I came looking for death,' he admitted. 'But not the death you offer. That was not specified.'

'But understood by nature of the Pact.'

'Not by me. I've never heard of any pact. I sought death as a warrior seeks it — in combat with my enemies.'

'Such an end will be yours. Yield now and I will inject you. You will feel no pain. You will float in a world of dreams in which everything you desire will be yours. A decade of subjective time.' The mandibles closed tighter on Varl's wrists. *'It is illogical for you to refuse.'*

'But human.' Varl snarled as he strained to push apart the curved menace. 'And you could be lying.'

'No. I do not lie.'

'How can you be certain that things are as you say?'

'The contact of minds tells me.' A pause then, *'It is not in the nature of the Vazela to enjoy pain.'*

'Then why give it? The threat is often worse than the execution.'

Varl felt the pressure on his wrists lessen a little.

Air rushed into his lungs as a shift of the thing's legs eased the constriction of his chest. A predator with a conscience — the thought illuminated the paradox. None who preyed on others could afford such a luxury but, if such a predator could read minds, appreciate and even vicariously share the fear and pain of the victim — what then?

On civilised worlds meat-animals were herded away out of sight, slaughtered in secret places, the meat disguised before serving. The conscience of the carnivore satisfied by lack of direct stimulus. As those addicted to the wearing of furs conveniently ignored the source from which they came.

A thing impossible for the Vazela to do — but they had found a solution to the problem.

The initial injection of what he had thought to be a paralysing venom. Teleman hadn't struggled once attacked, hadn't screamed as he was being devoured. And the nature of the feeding answered other questions.

'Potassium,' said Varl. 'The first injection neutralises it.'

'*Converts it,*' corrected the thing on his chest. '*It yields the subjective illusion I have mentioned.*'

That and more; a complex chemistry that activated the actual liquidisation of flesh and muscle. The brain would go first to be sucked from the skull by adapted appendages. Then the rest until nothing remained but the skin and skeleton. A dried husk to be discarded as a spider would discard the drained carcass of a beetle or a fly.

'The Pact,' said Varl. 'Tell me of that.'

'*The Scandhar came. They met the Vazela. There was fighting and many died. Then peace was made. They would cease to hunt us for our skins. We would help them with their machines and other needs. In return they gave us the disposal of their dead and dying.*'

Food delivered on a plate and 'dying' would include all due for execution for having broken any of a host of laws. A neat arrangement.

Varl said, 'You ride in the ships, right?' The creature's acknowledgement confirmed the state of the autopsy victims. 'What are your duties?' He blinked at the response. 'You mean you actually handle the operation of the vessel?'

'In many ways, yes. We are able to sense certain dangers and to guard against them. We are also good at other duties.'

The coordination of the armament and defensive shield.

The ability to avoid the attentions of the four-dimensional killer. No wonder the raiders could operate with such assurance in the Drift.

'Would you help me?' Varl added, quickly. 'We could make a personal pact. I want to get a ship and you can help me run it. It's better than guarding a roof,' he urged. 'The Scandhar don't own you, do they?'

'They feed me.'

'So would I.' The dead wouldn't care and the dying would be none of his own. 'A deal?' Varl forced conviction into his mind, assurance, trust. 'What is your name? You have a name?' The reply sounded like a number. 'Forten, right? Well, Forten, will you help me?'

'*I will be fed?*'

'Yes. I promise.'

'*Now? You came to die and have been spared. It is only fair to give me another.*'

A sacrifice to prove his sincerity; to lie or demure was to invite the pointed mandibles into his throat.

Varl rose as the creature backed away to melt into the umber shadows. Crossing to the edge of the roof he fastened the rope and slid down it to the barred window. Chatto caught him as he landed on the external ledge. Burchard helped him to the floor.

Koslenko said, 'Well?'

'It's all arranged.' Varl told them of the plan he had made with the women. 'Just get busy on those ropes. We'll need them strong and long. Where's Kendrick?'

He lay huddled at the far end of the room; a man wrapped in isolation. He stirred as Varl touched his shoulder, fear apparent in his eyes.

'Kurt?'

'I need you,' said Varl. 'Up on the roof.

There are things I don't understand. You can explain them to me.'

'On the roof? No. I — '

'It could be important,' Varl hauled the man to his feet. 'I'll go up first and you follow. I'll pull you up by the rope.' He urged him towards the window. 'Chatto will help you.'

'No!' Kendrick screamed, struggling against Varl's grip. 'I won't go! You can't make me!'

He slumped as Varl sent his fist to the side of his neck. A blow that numbed and stopped the noise. As Chatto stared his surprise Varl said, 'Send him up after me. Don't waste time.'

'Trouble?'

'No. Just do as I say.'

Again Varl reached the crenellations, avoiding the bells to stand, the rope in his hands, muscles bunching as he hauled up Kendrick's dead weight. The man stirred as Varl laid him on the roof.

'No!' He reared upright, eyes wild, 'Dear God, no!'

'You know what's up here.' Varl was grim. 'You couldn't have been a slave so long and ridden the ships without knowing about the Vazela. Yet you never mentioned them. You didn't warn me what I could be running into. Why?'

Ten years of slavery in which his spirit had been broken, his spine turned into jelly. The whip that had torn his body had warped his brain. Things too unpleasant to remember had been washed from his memory. Ghosts now resurrected to fill his mind with horrific fears.

'Please!' Kendrick cowered, hands lifted to mask his face, body redolent with the sweat of terror. 'Please don't hurt me! I'll do anything! Please!'

'Up!' Varl lifted the man, removed the rope, half-carried him towards the umber shadows, the creature patiently waiting. To apologise would add insult to injury, instead he tried to explain. 'I've made a promise and it has to be kept. One of us has to go and you're the logical choice. You for the rest — and you're the one who can most easily be spared. Try to understand. But it won't hurt. I promise you that.'

One fulfilled with another now. Harder,

this time, bringing a merciful oblivion. Varl put him down in the shadows, proof of his given word.

'Here,' he whispered. 'Here, damn you — come and feed.'

23

High on the wall the window was a patch of umber glow, one bearing the silhouette of a man; Jac Zuber whose nerves were near breaking.

'Kurt!' His voice, barely restrained, held the elements of a shout. 'Something's out here. God!'

Varl loped towards him, gripping the rope that hung down from the bars, swarming up it to catch at a metal upright, his free hand darting towards Zuber's wrist, halting the movement of his hand.

'Hold it!'

'It's out there! A thing like the one which — '

'One of the Vazela.' Varl was curt. 'I know. It's a friend.'

'A what?' Zuber stared his disbelief. 'After what one of its kind did to Teleman?'

'We need it.' Varl released Zuber's wrist

adding: 'Teleman could have been killed by a dog or a tiger and neither would have been as gentle. Forten's a friend. We need the help it can give. Don't let the way it looks scare you.' He thrust his arm through the window, leaning against the bars. Beneath his fingers he felt the softness of fur, the touch of a palp.

'*Dawn is near. If your plan is to work you must delay no longer.*'

'I know. Thanks.' Varl turned to Zuber. 'Give me your hand. Touch it. Let it touch you. Open your mind.' As the other hesitated he snarled. 'Damn it, man, you're supposed to be a scientist. If you're scared of blood why join us?'

He felt a momentary resistance then, as Zuber yielded, he heard the sudden, startled intake of the other's breath.

Patiently he waited then again touched the creature's body.

It moved as it clung spider-like to the wall; swaying as if about to spring.

'Forten?'

'*He was disturbed but he is calm now. He accepts as you have accepted.*'

'While you work with us you are one of

us. All will accept.'

'*You must cease to delay. The dawn —* '

'I know,' Varl broke contact. To Zuber he said, 'Lower the rope and drop down to the street. Twitch it when you land. Forten will tie with you. Have the others make contact when they arrive. If you are spotted try to bluff. If that doesn't work fight like hell. Forten will help.'

'What about the women?'

'If they arrive in time they come with us. If not — '

Varl shrugged.

'They get left behind. Like Kendrick?'

'Forget him.' Varl had no time or inclination to give explanations. 'Now move, damn you! Move!'

Another climbed to the window as Zuber slipped through the opening. As he moved on in turn Chatto replaced him.

'If you get delayed, Kurt, I'll move directly towards the field, where should I hold up to give you a chance of joining us?'

'There's a building with a pointed roof. Stay on the city side. Don't wait too long.'

Chatto lifted a hand in salute as he passed through the opening. Varl watched as he dropped out of sight then slid down the inner rope to the floor of the prison. The door was thick and muffled external sound. Burchard raised his head from where he had pressed his ear to the panel.

'Nothing.' He sounded bleak. 'I guess they couldn't make it —'

'There's still time.' Varl listened in turn, hearing a dull pounding, a thump, a metallic scratching. 'They're here!'

The door opened inward and he stood behind it, crushing the panel with his hands as it threatened to crush him against the wall. Light shone through it, illuminating Burchard's face, his naked body. Shining too on the men gathered beneath the window.

'Thank God!' Edallia ran into the room. Blood stained her gown, her arm, the hand holding a sharpened table knife. 'We're in time. Hurry!' She stepped aside as the other women followed her. To Burchard's question she snapped, 'We were delayed. A visitor. Then we ran into a nosey guard.' She lifted the blood stained knife. 'I took care of the bitch but others are following. Get that door shut. Jam it somehow. Hurry!'

'Wait!' Varl looked around the edge of the panel. 'How many?'

'Following us? Three, I think. They decided we weren't contagious. Get that door shut!'

'No.' Varl ducked behind it. 'Let them come in.'

They came with a pad of booted feet, tall, armed, bright in their armour. Each held a laser gun cradled in her arms, the weapons topped with the slender tubes of flashlights. The beams sliced the air, illuminating potential targets. As they levelled Varl thrust shut the door.

One turned, startled, crying out as Varl knocked up her laser gun, gripping her wrist and turning her arm as he ducked behind it. A savage jerk and he felt the elbow yield with a snap of bone. A chop of his stiffened hand and she fell.

Before she had reached the ground he was on another, right hand rising, the fingers and palm bent backward, the heel slamming against her nose, smashing it, driving splinters of bone up through the sinus cavities and into the brain.

Burchard had taken care of the remaining guard.

'Quick!' Varl stooped, ripped free a helmet, threw it at Edallia. 'Change. Become a guard. You too, Sylvia, Anne.' They were the right size. 'Hurry!'

'Our hair!' Sylvia Kiouza touched her raven locks. 'We'd never get away with it.'

For answer Varl snatched the knife she carried and hacked at the blonde tresses of the dead guard. Tucked beneath the helmet they covered the woman's natural hair and fringed her face with gold. Stripped, dressed in the dead woman's armour, she would pass in a dim light. Anne the same. Edallia hefted her laser gun.

'Maybe I should stay until the last in case of trouble.'

'I'll do that.' Varl took the weapon from her hands and examined it. 'Get to the window and join the rest. Did you bring a rope? Good. Tie it to the other bar. When you reach the ground do what Zuber tells you to. Obey him without question.' He looked at the other two women. 'No firing. No matter what you see don't shoot. Now move!'

He waited by the door as shadowy figures moved towards the window, climbed up towards it, became silhouettes that vanished to be replaced by others. The last, Burchard, called softly down to him,

'All down, Kurt. Get over here.'

He caught the laser gun as Varl threw it towards him, handed it back as he reached the bars. A wriggle and he was through the opening, was headed downward, the rope sighing through his hands. Varl waited until he was well towards the ground then followed. The ground slammed against his feet and he straightened, gun at the ready as he looked around.

The area was clear, an empty stretch illuminated by the pre-dawn haze and a scatter of lights that thickened towards the field. He stared at them, remembering details he had gained from his rooftop inspections. A street, a junction too well lit for comfort. An alley that ran behind tall, featureless houses. The building with the pointed roof. Beyond it lay the field, the ships, the means of escape.

'Here.' He handed Edallia the gun. 'We're a group of chiros being taken for some duty somewhere. Loading or cleaning a vessel. Where's Forten?'

'Over here.' A woman turned from where it squatted, a dazed expression on her face. 'No, I can't believe it. I . . . ' She shook her head. 'I've met aliens before but this is wild.'

'Without it we're stuck.' Varl moved to where it waited. Touched it. Asked questions and listened to the answers. To Edallia he said, 'You are in charge of the detail. You are escorting us to the repair sheds — number eight. It's on the left of the field as we approach. Make directly towards it. The ship we want has just been serviced. We are to complete the cleaning,'

'Name?'

Varl reached for the vazela. 'The *Gillian*.'

'Just like that?' Edallia sounded dubious. 'We simply walk on the field, head for the repair sheds, reach the ship and climb aboard? It sounds too easy.'

'So's murder.' Varl was impatient, 'All you need do is to pull a trigger.'

'It could be a trap,' Zuber shared her lack of conviction. 'That damned thing could be leading us right into it.'

'If so it'll be the first to die.' Varl was blunt. 'Have you a better plan? No? Then let's go!'

He fell into line with the other men, walking as slaves would walk; a time-consuming shuffle, head lowered, muscles lax. Edallia took the lead, strutting, laser-gun in her arms. Sylvia and Anne took up stations to either side and at the rear the other women before them at the end of the middle column. A position that, ostensibly, allowed them to burn down any opposition but which also yielded an open field of fire to either flank.

Forten loped at the rear, an alien dog herding sheep.

The street enclosed them, the junction with its bright, betraying lights approaching with every step. The mouth of the circling alley gaped to the left and, like a scuttling shadow, the vazela raced towards it.

'Follow,' Varl called to Edallia without raising his head, 'Follow where it leads.'

For a moment she hesitated then saw the betraying glint of metal from beneath an upcurved roof. A watchful guard or guards, armed, poised for action. Saw too the shape of the alien, rearing, palps moving as if in urgent summons. Without breaking step she moved towards it, feeling sweat break out on face and body, a sudden relief as shadows closed around her.

'A trap.' The man walking beside Varl voiced his fear. Duggan, once top of his class, now out of it. 'Zuber was right. They're guiding us, making us take the path they want us to follow. In this maze we can't tell where the hell we're going.'

'Watch your mouth!' If he was right whisper-mikes could be tracking them and pick up the betrayal. If wrong he was still damaging morale. 'We'll make it.'

'Like Kendrick?'

'He's dead.' Varl was harsh. 'His life bought you the chance to save your own.

Throw it away if you want but don't make the rest of us pay for your lack of guts.'

The alley twisted, the blank-faced buildings yielding to others, smaller, set with groined windows and ornamental tiles. Light blazed at the far end, beyond it lay the field, the sheds and shapes of grounded vessels. Guards stood beneath the suspended globes looking towards the column as it advanced. One stepped forward, hand uplifted.

'Halt!' She waited as Edallia obeyed. 'What is your business?'

'Party for the *Gillian*. Cleaning detail.'

'Your name?'

'Mirza Walsh.' Edallia spoke without hesitation. 'Aspirant captain. Yours?'

'Field officer Leman. What are women doing among your chiros?'

'I'm taking them to the vivarium.'

'Across the field?'

Edallia said, patiently, 'The chiros get dropped off at the ship then the women will be taken where they are to go. If you think it odd then complain to the Marshal. She will be most amused at having being woken at this hour. Still, that's your problem, I'm just obeying orders.'

'You know the Marshal?'

'Liza Olenya?' Edallia smiled. 'Yes, I know her. We've been very close at times.'

'I see,' The officer looked to either side, at her guards, at the column she had halted. She drew in her breath as a tawny shape seemed to materialise from the umber shadows. 'Yours?'

'Mine.' Edallia dropped a hand to caress the creature's fur. 'When I gain my command it will ride with me.' She let irritation edge her tone. 'Now, with your permission, I'd like to get on with what has to be done. May I pass?'

Duggan gusted his relief as the officer stepped back, nodding. 'Done it,' he said. 'By God, we've done it!'

Varl wasn't so sure.

24

He tensed as they walked on, the hatefully familiar jerking of his nerves a warning that all was not as it seemed. Guards had been at the junction with the lights, more at the point they had just passed, things he hadn't noticed at his rooftop examinations. There had been lights, then, true, but not as many. And why had it been decided the women weren't contagious? What had happened when the dead guards had failed to report?

Behind him Chatto said, 'There's the ship. Over to the left.'

The *Gillian*, resting before wide, open doors. The new-born day had paled the sky and in the strengthening light the hull glowed with a warm, golden promise. A scatter of chiros worked to one side of it, moving with slow deliberation as they raked and smoothed the dirt. Old men with prominent ribs, collars circling scrawny throats, kilts wrapped around withered loins.

Kilts!

Varl pretended to stumble, looking back at the guard post, seeing the officer gesture to someone out of view. Two others, guns at the ready, had straightened and were staring at the party.

Varl said, urgently, 'Something's wrong. Get the women up here, mix them among us. Pass the word to Anne and Sylvia. Edallia, head to the right.'

'The ship's to the left.'

'They're waiting for us. They know we aren't what we seem.' Chiros wore kilts and he and the other men were naked. Something the field officer must have noticed but she had made no comment. Which meant she must have been acting under orders; delaying them before allowing them to pass. Varl said, 'They won't open fire for fear of hurting the women. They'll try to freeze us. Don't give them time to close the trap.'

'Three guns,' said Edallia. 'Against how many?'

'You'll be firing first. Once some are down we'll get their guns.' Varl looked towards the *Gillian*, the shed behind it, at other ships lying on the field. Any could provide an escape but all could turn into a prison if they weren't immediately operational. 'Swing out and around so as to come in from the far side.' To the others he said, 'When I give the word scatter and run. You know what needs to be done.'

Kill, fight, kill again for to hesitate was to die. A lesson they had learned the hard way and put into practice more than once. The others, the few remaining from the traditional military academies, would learn or they would go down to stain the dirt with their blood and sinew; gasping out their lives beneath an alien sun.

'March!' Anne, moving forward, plied her whip, voice raised in apparent anger. 'Move, damn you! Move!'

A woman screamed, another stumbled catching at a man as she staggered forward. For a moment there was confusion during which the party broke its ordered direction and turned to run in disorder towards the space beyond the ship. Yards covered in seconds, reversed as the bulk of the hull masked them from the guards at the post.

Others were waiting.

A dozen of them standing in a casual grouping against the hull, weapons cradled in their arms. As they leveled Edallia opened fire, the others following, all three sending a hail of searing bolts of energy to burn flesh, heat armour, turn golden tresses into smoking flame.

'Now!'

Varl was running even as he shouted, racing to one side, throwing himself down as a gun swung towards him. He felt the burn of its blast on his naked back as he rose, his left hand knocking the barrel upwards, his right, stiffened, sending its fingers like blunted spears into the pits of the vivid blue eyes.

'The shed!' He snatched up the weapon, fired to end the screaming of the blinded guard, again to bring down another who had turned to run. 'Get into the shed!'

'Why not the ship?' Chatto, a gun in his hand, blood running from a charred hole in his side, snapped the question,

'They expected us. There'll be more in

312

the shed. Unless we take them out they'll burn us down as we try to pass through the lock.'

'We could be trapped.'

'That or dead.' Varl fired, ran, fired again. 'Come on!'

The guards had gone; dead or running for their lives. A few naked bodies lay among them, some groaning, others still. Duggan was among them; the trap he had feared had taken his life.

Varl ignored him as he did the rest. To lose time now was to lose their only chance. The doors of the shed were open before him, the bulk of enigmatic machines illuminated by brilliant cones of light thrown from suspended sources. Some chiros ran like hens before the attack of a fox and, in the corner, he saw the glint of metal, the movement of a plume.

Decoration that gave all the warning he needed.

The plume vanished in a puff of smoke. The helmet beneath it, reflecting the beam of the laser, shone like a star. The face beneath that turned into something from nightmare as he burned the skin, the meat, the blood to leave only charred and smoking bone.

'In! Scatter! Get them all!'

Hunt them down before they could assemble. Hit them before they could realise they faced a different brand of man than their broken chiros. Burn them. Destroy them. Take their lives, their guns, their power.

Within seconds the interior of the shed had become a shrieking abattoir, the air heavy with the stench of blood, of burning, of heated and smoking metal.

Then, abruptly, all was still.

'That's the last.' Edallia turned a slumped figure with her foot. She had remained untouched; the uniform she wore had confused the attacking guards. 'What next?'

'Check our losses. Get the other women into disguise.'

'Why waste time?'

'We can't afford a mistake. The guards will hesitate to fire on those they think to be their own. We could even pull a bluff if we have to.' He snapped his impatience. 'Don't argue, just do it.'

Anne had been burned on one arm. Sylvia waited impassively as Madden staunched the blood from a wound on her thigh. Minor hurts matched by those borne by the other women; the guards had hesitated to destroy those of their own sex. With the men they hadn't been so gentle.

'Three dead.' Chatto made the report. 'Seven hurt, two badly.'

'Can they fight? Move?' Varl nodded at the answer. 'Good. They can stand watch and we'll help them at the last. Any chiros?'

A score of them stood where they had been herded to the rear of the shed. Cleaners, polishers, sweepers, oilers — none had been allowed to gain experience with tools.

'Get their kilts,' said Varl. 'And find something to cut free these damned collars.'

'Theirs?'

'Ours. Just cut them so they can be dumped when we want. 'Don't discard them yet.'

Chatto nodded, understanding. 'You're going to use the chiros to emulate us. Naked, collared — why not use a few as guards?'

'Pick three. Crop the dead women's

315

hair — you know what to do. Make sure their guns won't work.'

Varl moved towards the open doors and cautiously looked outside. The field seemed deserted but guards could be hiding behind the bulk of hulls and other ships could be on their way. The port of the *Gillian* was open and he stared at it, wondering if guards with guns waited inside.

If so they would have to be lured out. Forten was nowhere in sight; the creature had disappeared when the first gun had been fired,

Zuber had noticed its absence.

'How do we operate without it?'

'We'll find a way.' Varl turned and looked over the shed. The chiros, naked, stood huddled together, three of their number looking ridiculous in guards uniform, shorn hair hanging over lined faces. They held their guns as if afraid they would be burned. 'Let's get assembled. Time is against us.'

A man cut free his collar and Varl pushed it closed again. The kilt flapped at his loins and he missed the freedom of nudity. As he missed the comforting weight of a gun.

'Now!'

He moved out, skin crawling to an anticipated blast, the others following, Edallia and two of the others driving them as if they had been cattle. A close bunch that masked the extra weapons the women carried. From a distance their kilts would signal them to be the shed-chiros under the command of victorious guards.

Deliberately they moved away from the ship.

Behind, in the shed, Burchard counted seconds.

'Out!' The whip sang in his hand, 'Out, damn you! Get into the ship!'

A mistake; chiros did not give orders. One corrected by Natalie, by Eunice and Daphne. Women dressed as guards, armed, their whips a stinging menace.

'Out! Out and to the ship! Move!'

A bunch of men naked but for their collars. The same as had passed the guard post accompanied by the same three women wearing uniforms stolen from murdered guards. The intruders, victorious, coming to take over the ship.

The moment those inside had been waiting for.

They streamed through the port, taking their time, confident their numbers and weapons would bring immediate obedience,

'Halt!' Their officer widened her eyes at their unpardonable insolence. Mistaking their rush towards her as an attack and not the desire for protection it was. 'Halt, I say! Guards! Fire!'

The surrogate women first; they carried guns. Then the hapless chiros who fell like reaped corn, bleeding, charred, their collars glowing red. A moment of victory turned instantly into defeat as Varl snatched a gun from where it hung at Edallia's waist.

'Get them!'

Energy burned from the golden hull, hit the uniformed shapes, sent them to the dirt. A vicious crossfire from within the shed and from the group to one side. Before the last had hit the dirt Varl was running to the port, had reached it, was through it, gun ready as he roved the unfamiliar confines of the ship.

'Kurt?'

'Nothing. It's deserted.' He pushed past Edallia and back to the port. Burchard came limping from the shed, a limp figure slung over a shoulder. Another followed him, the last. 'In. Get inside.'

'The port?'

'I'll take care of it.' Varl looked outside as the others moved deeper into the vessel. 'Forten! Forten, damn you, where are you?'

Feeding, sucking the juice from one of the initial dead. It rose to glide like a racehorse over the dirt, reaching the port, passing through it as Varl slammed it shut. A creature with the agility of a spider and the self-preservation of a cat. A palp touched Varl's hand.

'*Are we ready to leave?*'

'Yes.'

'*Get into the control room. Sit in the pilot's chair.*'

It was big, enveloping, a structure to hold with gentle firmness. Varl sank into it and felt the touch, the voice in his mind.

'*Think — I will accomplish.*'

A living computer. One with sharper senses than any human, its limbs and brain attuned to multiple tasks. While it remained in contact with the pilot it would act on given orders.

'Up!' Varl almost screamed his urgency. 'Up and away.'

From Gorm, the women who ruled it, the danger it presented. A world that vanished as the hydee twisted space, hurling the *Gillian* into relative safety, leaving it to drift. A period of quiescence during which those it carried settled themselves. Became a crew again.

'We made it,' Edallia looked at the screens, the orbs drifting in the umber haze. At the unfamiliar universe all around them. 'We got away.'

'So far.' Varl leaned forward, breaking contact. 'We were lucky.'

'I'd call it something else.' Edallia shrugged. 'What does it matter? We've a ship, the answer to the raiders, Forten who can get us back. Everything Nasir Kalif wanted.'

'So?'

She drew in her breath, inflating her chest, breasts thrusting against the scaled armour she still wore. A warrior-queen wearing silk and metal.

'So let's go home.'

Varl said, 'To what? A reward? A pension? A medal and a thank you and a kick up the butt? I want more.'

'Kalif will give it to you.'

'I'd rather help myself.' He gestured at the screens. 'Look at what's out there — a universe for the taking. All we need is determination.'

'And men,' she reminded. 'Women too — where do you find your extra crew?'

'In the Drift. The Spiral.' Varl looked at where it lay, a blur against the umber haze. 'It's all there, ships, supplies, men and women — all frozen in stasis. Everything we need.' Kreutzal too, maybe, the secrets he could have learned. All the loot accumulated over the ages. 'A chance,' he said. 'The best we'll ever get. I'm going to take it.'

And so would they all.

THE END

FIFTY DAYS TO DOOM
THE DEATH ZONE
THE STELLAR LEGION
STARDEATH
TOYMAN

We do hope that you have enjoyed reading this large print book.

Did you know that all of our titles are available for purchase?

We publish a wide range of high quality large print books including:
Romances, Mysteries, Classics
General Fiction
Non Fiction and Westerns

Special interest titles available in large print are:
The Little Oxford Dictionary
Music Book, Song Book
Hymn Book, Service Book

Also available from us courtesy of Oxford University Press:
Young Readers' Dictionary
(large print edition)
Young Readers' Thesaurus
(large print edition)

For further information or a free brochure, please contact us at:
Ulverscroft Large Print Books Ltd.,
The Green, Bradgate Road, Anstey,
Leicester, LE7 7FU, England.
Tel: (00 44) **0116 236 4325**
Fax: (00 44) **0116 234 0205**

Other titles in the
Linford Mystery Library:

SEND FOR DR. MORELLE

Ernest Dudley

Mrs. Lorrimer telephones Doctor Morelle claiming that she's in imminent mortal danger. In the morning her orange drink was poisoned, then she'd found a deadly snake in her bed and now toxic gas is emanating from the chimney and into the room! But is she really in danger? Is she mad — or perhaps feigning madness? Dutifully, Doctor Morelle sets off to the woman's house with Miss Frayle, his long-suffering assistant, who will soon begin to wish she'd stayed behind . . .

DR. MORELLE ELUCIDATES

Ernest Dudley

Dr. Morelle expounds on seven puzzling cases in his inimitable manner. For *The Case of the Man Who Was Too Clever*, the doctor and his assistant Miss Frayle investigate the murder of an actress, whose dying screams are the clue to her death. Whilst in *The Case of the Clever Dog*, a murder is committed in the doctor's presence, but man's best friend is the clue in finding the killer . . .

THE G-BOMB

John Russell Fearn

The cleverest man on Earth, Jonas Glebe, becomes the unwitting tool of a baleful intelligence. His invention, the G-Bomb, should bring riches to himself and his daughter Margaret — instead it brings death and a deadly threat to mankind . . . Val Turner knows the danger, but he's imprisoned — framed for Margaret's murder. His release comes too late to prevent the cataclysm engulfing the world. But fate decrees that he saves a strange little man from drowning, and thereby changes destiny . . .

THE VANISHING MAN

Sydney J. Bounds

Popular novelist and secret agent Alec Black is on an undercover mission on Mars. The Martian colonists are preparing for a major offensive against earth and someone is stirring up war-fever. Black must try to prevent it, or the whole system will be engulfed in atomic war. When Black finds himself shadowed by a man who, when confronted, vanishes into thin air, his investigation turns into his strangest case and very soon he's plunged into a dimension of horror . . .

TOYMAN

E. C. Tubb

Space-wanderer Earl Dumarest is on the planet Toy, hoping he'll get information on the whereabouts of Earth, his lost home world. But nothing is given freely there and he must fight in the Toy Games to gain the information he needs. He's forced to be like a tin soldier in a vast nursery with a spoiled child in command — but there's nothing playful about the Games on Toy. Everything is only too real: pain, wounds, blood — and death . . .

THE PREMONITION

Drew Launay

Nostradamus lives . . . in his descendant Michael Dartson. On a journey to the homes of his ancestors, a strangely bewitching woman shows him that the past is alive. Michael must experience the most traumatic moments of his forefathers' lives — rape, cannibalism, unspeakable violence. His infamous ancestor has set some terrible plan in motion — and Michael is only an instrument. The time is near. The horrors of the past are nothing compared to the evils of the future . . .